# FULL MOON LAGOON

*by*

Monica Nawrocki

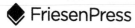
## FriesenPress

Suite 300 - 990 Fort St
Victoria, BC, Canada, V8V 3K2
www.friesenpress.com

**Copyright © 2015 by Monica Nawrocki**
All Illustrations copyrighted by Lisa Gibbons
First Edition — 2015

**ISBN**
978-1-4602-7713-3 (Hardcover)
978-1-4602-7714-0 (Paperback)
978-1-4602-7715-7 (eBook)

1. *Juvenile Fiction, Time Travel*
2. *Juvenile Fiction, Action & Adventure*
3. *Juvenile Fiction, Historical, Canada*

Distributed to the trade by The Ingram Book Company

# Table of Contents

This book is respectfully dedicated to the Nakatsui family

of Cortes Island, interned in 1942.

## CHAPTER 1
# TURTLE ISLAND

"Do you think anyone ever died doing this, Cat?"

I looked down at Hague Lake, and the buzzing in my ears started again. I took a big breath and a big step back from the ledge. Not a good place to get dizzy.

The jump was truly terrifying because I couldn't see where I'd hit the water. The rock bulged out so I had to take a run at it and fling myself blindly off the cliff. I didn't know that until I climbed up fifty feet and tried to convince my legs to carry my vital organs into midair in order to plunge into the lake at a spot my eyes couldn't even see.

My brain did not approve.

"I'm sure no one's died, Maddy," said Cat. "If they had, this would be *Tragedy Island*, not Turtle Island."

Cat lay behind me on a mossy rock. Her long, straight black hair looked blue in the bright August light. She gets her hair from her mom, Denise, who's Chinese. Cat's father, Lyle, isn't Chinese, but her mom always says the rest of them like him anyways. Family joke.

Cat Beaton is my best friend, even though she lives three ferry rides away in Vancouver. Her family has a cabin here, so we've spent every summer together since we were six. We're twelve now.

Her name isn't really Cat, by the way; it's Alicia Catherine, which she hates. First, she was Ally, then Ally Cat, and eventually it turned into Cat. She didn't seem to mind, and I've always thought she had rather cat-like qualities anyway: independent and not prone to emotional outbursts.

I think it's good to have a friend from away because I've lived on Cortes Island most of my life, and sometimes

I forget to notice the things that Cat notices. Like how beautiful the ocean is when the sun scatters diamonds across it. Or how amazing the old growth trees are. Or how clean the lake is.

I looked around for more little rocks to drop over the edge.

"What's with the stones, Maddy?" asked Cat.

"I want to make sure all I hear is pebbles hitting the water. I do *not* want to hear pebbles crashing into the rock and plunging to their deaths."

I looked at Cat and sighed. She was turning a lovely golden brown in the sun while I was sizzling like bacon. My shoulder-length red hair was about to frizz out; ten minutes more and I'd look like a circus clown.

"Do you know how hard it is to climb back down from here in bare feet?" Cat asked.

"As hard as climbing up?" I snapped.

"Incorrect, Smartass. It's harder. Because of the shame."

"We're not climbing, we're jumping. Don't rush me." I backed up a few steps and made like a sprinter on the starting line. Then my heart accelerated until it tripped over itself.

I inched forward for another look, then squinted at the beach across the lake. Voices floated over the water. They sounded like humans, but they looked like ants.

"And for sure, this is the right spot?" I asked, munching nervously on my fingernail.

"Maddy! We've watched people jump from here a million times!"

"Ya, but . . ."

Before I could finish, Cat trotted by me and flung herself off the cliff. I froze. My eyes and ears were wide open as I pictured her pinwheeling to her death. I exhaled when I heard the splash, then froze again, waiting for her to resurface.

"Come on, Maddy. It's awesome!" Cat called.

"Are you out of the way?"

"Yes!"

With my heart yammering wildly, I backed up a few steps, then ran and jumped out as far as I could. I remembered to keep my arms in tight but forgot to point my toes, so I slapped my size eights painfully as I entered the lake at a zillion miles an hour and plunged through the cold. I opened my eyes, looked up toward the sunshine, and followed my trail of bubbles. When my head broke the surface, I gulped air and whooped a happy echo across the water.

We swam back toward the beach. I couldn't decide which was better—that I hadn't killed myself or that I could finally say I'd done the Big Jump.

On the white sand, I dried off, slathered myself in sunscreen lotion, and then got Cat to do my back. She made a crack about playing "Connect the Dots" with the freckles on my shoulders, so I asked her if she needed a chair to help her reach.

Cat's nearly a head shorter than me. She's smaller than most of her classmates and I'm taller than mine, so together we look like a mismatched set of salt and pepper shakers. My out-of-control hair doesn't help either.

"So, what was going on when I called yesterday?" Cat asked.

"Another fight with Grunt," I shrugged.

Grunt is my stepdad. His name is actually Grant, but Grunt suits him better. He's a software designer, so he can work anywhere, even on this little island—although he complains constantly about our wonky high-speed inter*not*.

"Now what?" Cat sounded slightly impatient.

"Why'd you say it like that?" I asked.

"You fight with him every day. Why don't you just stay out of his way?"

"Have you ever lived with someone in a wheelchair? He's in everyone's way all the time, and he couldn't care less!"

Cat rolled gracefully onto her side and looked at me. "How do you know he doesn't care? Should he apologize every time someone has to go around him?"

I sat up and glared at her. "You know it's not about the chair. Grunt doesn't like me. He looks at me like I'm something nasty he found in the back of the fridge."

"Whatever," she said and rolled over again.

I laid down and let the sun melt my anger.

"What should we do tomorrow?" I asked finally. It was the third week of August, and I'd begun to panic at the thought of summer coming to an end. Time to start fun-cramming.

"I don't know. What's left on your crazy to-do list?" Cat asked.

"Well, we haven't gone lagoon diving at night, and we've been talking about that one for ages. I'll call you after I check the tide chart." I rummaged through my bag until I found my watch. "Oops. I have to go."

# CHAPTER 2
# THE EVIL TWIN

By the time I walked home, the sun had slipped behind the trees. The sky was deep blue with no sign of clouds. It looked like a good night for lagoon diving. The tide should be coming in around midnight, but since it changes by forty-five minutes every day, I'd have to check the tide chart.

The whole point of lagoon diving is to catch the fastest part of the incoming tide. As the lagoon fills, the water rushes through the narrow mouth really fast. The current below the surface is so strong that when you dive in you pop back up twenty feet away. Then you float out into the middle of the lagoon. It's better than a waterslide.

I was checking the tides on the computer when my grandmother walked into the house.

"Hey, Grandma," I called. I left the computer and followed her into the kitchen to help.

"How was your day, Sweetie?" Grandma asked as she put a box of groceries on the counter.

Before it went grey, my grandma's hair was red like mine. She calls my hair *fiery red*, and then she points to her own and says that *age changes fire to ash*. Plus, everyone says our eyes are the same green although, since Grandpa's death last winter, hers have lost their sparkle.

"I had a great day! Cat and I jumped off the big cliff on Turtle Island!" I put the eggs away.

Grandma looked at me, checking to see if I was serious or not. She frowned and shook her head.

"Thank you for not telling me you planned to do that, Madison," Grandma muttered as she rearranged the fridge to make more room.

Grandma used to be the one encouraging my sense of adventure, which she said was like her own. But since Grandpa died in November, Grandma's changed. For one thing, she worries more.

I stared after her as she left the kitchen. How did it feel for her to be on Cortes without Grandpa? He grew up on this island. Everything must be a reminder of him and his stories.

I went back to the computer and changed screens. What luck! Full moon. High tide. Clear skies.

I called Cat. We were making plans for sneaking out when I remembered The Evil Twin. "Wait a minute," I said. "Where's Draggin?"

"I don't know. Why?" Cat asked.

I rolled my eyes. How could she ask me that? Cat's twin brother had sabotaged many of our adventures in the planning stage. He's a skulker, he is. An eavesdropper. A blackmailer.

Draggin's about two minutes older and half an inch taller than Cat but not nearly as good-looking, which we point out to him as often as possible. He keeps his black hair short because when it gets long—as it usually does by the end of the summer—it gets a bit, shall we say, fluffy.

Cat's parents believe that if the twins stick together, they'll be safe from danger. Especially their mother, whose family gets together every single weekend in the city. In her opinion, together means better, so we use her weird adult logic to our advantage: we plan whatever we want to do and then sell it to Cat's parents by including Duncan—"draggin" him everywhere we want to go. That's how he got his nick name, which he thinks is *Dragon*. Rather naïve, wouldn't you say?

We told him it was Dragon because he was born in that year on the Chinese zodiac. Of course, only Cat and I know that it's really *Draggin*—which is what we write on notes to each other, but if anyone else in the family might see, we use *Dragon*. Everybody happy.

"Well, I don't trust him," I said into the phone. "Let's meet at the store to make our plan."

"No way. I just got comfy in the hammock."

"Okay, but make sure he's not hiding somewhere, listening. Or watching."

"Trust me, the joint is empty. I haven't heard a sound since I got home," Cat said.

We made arrangements to meet at the end of Cat's driveway at eleven thirty that night. She could sneak right out the front door because her parents went to bed early and Draggin slept like a rock. I wouldn't have any trouble getting out my bedroom window and into the woods. If anyone did look into my room, they'd see Pillow Maddy in my bed.

I hung up, found a dry bathing suit, and packed a bag. When the phone rang a few minutes later, I picked it up to find one angry Cat on the other end.

"We're busted!" she said.

"What? By who?"

"Draggin, of course! The little geek was bird-watching in the back yard and saw me on the deck with the phone. He lip-read my side of the conversation through his stupid binoculars and figured it out. You better get over here and help me with damage control."

Draggin was an expert lip-reader.

His hearing loss gave him far too many ways to screw up our lives. It all started with his parents, actually. With the possibility of his hearing getting worse, they decided to fully equip Draggin for life with or without hearing. As a result, he could hear a bit without his hearing aids; he could hear pretty well with them; and he could speak, sign, and, of course, lip-read. It wasn't the first time he'd used his extra skills—or "super powers" as he called them—to foul up our plans.

I arrived, out of breath, to find Draggin smirking smugly and Cat stomping around the deck. He looked more like a cat than she did at the moment.

"Okay, you two—what's going on?" I pulled up a deck chair and dropped into it.

"The little snoop says he'll rat us out unless we let him come."

"What?" My head snapped toward Draggin. "Why?"

He shrugged. "I want to come."

Cat and I exchanged a look; our weirdness detectors were activated. Draggin, a weak swimmer, didn't really like the water. Why would he want to come? Why wasn't he blackmailing us for Cat's allowance, like usual?

"What's your game, Mister?" I poked my finger at him and scowled.

"Nothing. We all go or no one goes." He looked unconcerned, but I smelled a bluff.

"Fine. No one, then. Come on, Cat, let's go." I got up from my chair and started to leave.

"That's it?" Draggin asked.

"That's it," I said and then turned back to face him. "Unless you tell us what's really going on."

He jutted out his lower teeth and growled: his version of a dragon. I rolled my eyes at him.

"Well?" I asked, tapping my toe.

He stared past me, frowning and blushing at the same time. "During the day, there are people watching, and I'm afraid I won't be able to swim across the current to the rock, and I'll get carried past like the little kids do. I want to try it at night when there's no one around."

Cat and I looked at each other again: bull-crap detectors now activated.

He added his last argument. "Don't worry, Maddy, you won't have to save me. I just don't want to look . . . like a wimp." He blushed again and looked at the deck. The breeze lifted his soft black hair and ruffled it like the feathers of a baby ostrich.

I had been thinking I might have to save him, but he was right; he wouldn't drown. He'd just get carried into the lagoon and miss the diving rock.

I raised an eyebrow at Cat, who had returned to the hammock. When she shrugged, I turned back to Draggin. He pushed out his lower lip and blew a quick blast of air up at his forehead to get the feathers out of his eyes.

"Okay," I said. "You can come tonight, but you're sworn to secrecy about this and any other adventures you poke your big nose into for the rest of the summer. Deal?"

"Deal. By the way, the tide will actually be highest in a couple of days—"

I cut him off. "I know. If you're coming, you do it our way and don't drive us crazy with your 'little-known facts.' This is an adventure, not school."

The walking encyclopedia shrugged and left the deck. He reads more books in a month than I've read in my life.

I turned to Cat. "Will he keep his mouth shut?"

Cat, swinging gently in the hammock, lifted her hand, made a fist, and bobbed it at me: American Sign Language for "yes."

Sign language was the twins' first language, and it has come in handy many times. Get it? Handy.

They've often been in the same class at school. Cat spends a lot of time daydreaming and then gets Draggin to sign answers to her when she needs them. Hanging out with them so much, I'd learned quite a few signs.

I poked her. "Are you sure we can trust him?"

Cat opened one eye. "Yup. I think he's serious about wanting to try it. Nice touch getting him hushed up for the rest of the summer. Does this mean you have something else planned?"

"Not yet, but I'm working on it."

# CHAPTER 3
# SLIPSTREAM

Around ten thirty, I put on my pyjamas and went out to say good night. Mom was sweating away in the kitchen where she'd been canning plums all evening. She wore a kerchief to keep her hair out of her eyes as she worked, but wisps of red frizz had escaped everywhere. She wore shorts and a sleeveless t-shirt. My mom is quite fit. For a mom. Judging by the pictures of my dad, I'd say I get my muscles from her.

I kissed her good night and asked where Grandma was.

"Out on the deck with her tea. And Dad's in his office." She didn't see me roll my eyes.

Grandma sat in her favourite chair and was wrapped in a blanket even though the evening was still t-shirt-and-shorts warm.

"Good night, Grandma." As I leaned over to kiss her, she brushed a tear from her cheek.

"Good night, Sweetie." She'd brought the framed picture of Grandpa from her room and set it beside her on the wooden table he'd made for her evening "deck sits." I missed his crooked smile and crinkly eyes.

Grandma reached up and patted my hand. "This was your grandpa's favourite time of day, between twilight and dark—called it 'magic time.' Of course, when he was growing up, there weren't even house lights—no electricity. Just lantern glow from each cabin." She nodded toward the scattered lights in the distance, then wiped another tear from her face. "He thought there was magic on this island, and not only at twilight. Believed in magic until the day he died. Used to tell me the craziest stories from when he was a boy here . . ."

I squeezed Grandma's hand and nodded. Grandpa always had stories about this "magic" island. Especially the lagoon. He was the one who taught me to lagoon dive, after insisting I start swimming lessons when I was really little.

After a couple of minutes, Grandma sat up straighter and gave me a sad smile. "You go on and have a good sleep, Sweetie. I'll see you in the morning."

I kissed her again and left. My heart felt crammed into my chest like feet in last year's shoes.

In his office, my stepdad sat hunched over his computer as usual. I stood watching him, wondering what to say. How could it be so complicated to say good night? I had tried to call him "Dad" a few times when he first moved in, but I couldn't do it. He looked annoyed when I called him Grant—so did Mom. So I stopped calling him anything at all. That works fine most of the time, but just saying "good night" without a name sounds kinda weird.

"You need something, Maddy?" Grunt asked.

"I came to say good night . . ." The end of the sentence fizzled away like the vapour trail from an airplane.

"Good night. Have a good sleep." He turned his attention back to the computer, and I escaped.

In my room, I prepared Pillow Maddy, just in case. Apart from the house catching fire, I couldn't imagine why anyone would come into my room. I changed into my bathing suit and pulled some clothes over top.

At 11:20 I eased open my window, tossed my bag out, and followed it. Without Grandpa around to do the yard work, the forest was busy trying to get into the house, which made it easy to get away without being seen.

I cut through the trees to the spot where Cat's driveway met the main road, and I crouched down in the salal bushes. As I waited for the twins, bat silhouettes hunted invisible mosquitoes above me. The moon, high and bright, let me save my flashlight battery for other adventures.

At 11:25 p.m.—according to Draggin's waterproof watch—the three of us started down the road toward the lagoon. On such a bright August night, I expected some traffic on the road, but we arrived without seeing anyone.

We walked out to the end of the sand spit that separated the lagoon from the Strait of Georgia. The moon threw a silver path along the surface of the water and painted the sky inky blue. The stars dimmed in the bright moonlight. I stood silently, soaking it in. House lights were scattered around the perimeter of the lagoon. About a dozen families enjoyed this amazing view.

At the mouth of the lagoon, the sea funnelled through the gap between the spit and the far shore. The conditions were perfect; the water rushed through the mouth with a force that gave me goose bumps. The big boulder that squatted in the middle of the mouth lay three-quarters underwater. At a real low tide, you could walk right out to it. The rock, which was the size of a minivan, sat a school bus length away from the spit, but the current between them could have swept any minivan away.

Draggin stood on the ocean side of the sand spit and squinted at the sailboats lined up along the government dock.

"Draggin, what are you doing?" Cat hissed.

"Just seeing if anyone's watching."

"They can't see us any better than we can see them. Get over here."

Draggin and I stood looking at the water while Cat found a spot for our clothes and towels above the high water mark.

I pointed across the mouth of the lagoon to the other shore. "See that really crooked arbutus tree?"

"Yes," Draggin said.

"When you get in, swim straight for that tree."

"But I'll go right past the rock!" he said.

"No, the current is really strong. If you aim there," I said, pointing at the tree, "you should end up there." I indicated the rock. "Cat will go first, then you, then me. If you can't get to the rock, don't worry. The current will carry you into the lagoon—it's not dangerous. If you do get nervous, yell, and I'll float out with you. Okay?"

"Okay," he said, but he already looked nervous. His lower lip protruded and he air-blasted the hair off of his forehead every five seconds.

Cat returned in her bathing suit and water shoes. Draggin and I walked to the rock Cat had chosen for our things, stripped down to our bathing suits, and switched footwear. As we approached the shoreline, Draggin suddenly stopped, and his hands flew to his ears.

"Oh, no," he cried. "I forgot to leave my aids at home. If I get water or sand in them, I'm dead."

We carefully placed them into the toe of Draggin's sneaker under his pile of clothes. Cat faced Draggin directly so he could read her lips easily. "If you need help, holler."

She waded up to her knees, already working hard against the current. Sparkling bioluminescence danced around her legs like hundreds of scuba-diving fireflies.

Draggin vibrated beside me, and I started to get nervous. What if he panicked? It's not so easy to float when you're busy freaking out.

Cat aimed herself at the arbutus tree on the opposite bank and plunged into the stream like a torpedo. She kept her head above water and stroked forward at the same rate that the current pushed her sideways. Once across, she reached for the rock and grabbed hold, still kicking her legs to get them out of the current. She caught her breath, pulled herself onto the ledge, and clambered up onto the top of the rock. She turned to face us and flashed the thumbs up.

"Ready?" I asked Draggin.

He nodded, but his breathing sounded short and choppy. I touched his arm so that he looked at me again. "Take a few big breaths first."

I'm a big believer in breathing. I mean, breathing and paying attention to it. In fourth grade our teacher taught us to breathe deeply as a calming technique, and it became a habit. It may be the only good habit I have. And it's doubly good because you can't do mindful breathing properly while chomping on your fingernails, and I'm a wicked bad nail-biter.

I chewed while Draggin took three breaths.

When he was calm, we walked out together. He tottered in the current and stepped back into the shallow water. On his second attempt, he glared at the arbutus tree and dove.

He was not as graceful as his sister, but he thrashed his way across the current with determined pulls. Cat stood on the lowest ledge she could find, ready to help him up and, in a few seconds, Draggin bounded onto the top of the rock, whooping victoriously.

I exhaled, suddenly aware of how tense I'd been. I waded into the water, dove into the stream, and swam hard through the current.

Soon, the three of us stood on the rock; the mini river rushed past. Riding the surface was like tobogganing down a gentle slope, but catching the slipstream below felt like riding a rocket!

I showed Draggin where to dive. Cat would go first, then Draggin, then me. We agreed to stay close together, just in case.

*How long do I wait after you dive?* he signed.

*You don't have to wait,* Cat signed back. *As soon as I'm in the water, I'm already gone.*

Draggin nodded. His excitement was starting to out-weigh his fear. He looked at me and asked, "Ready?" I nodded, and he turned back to Cat. *Go now*, he signed.

Cat dove immediately. She entered the water in a grace-ful arc. Then Draggin threw himself in head first, hitting the water with a big splash. I dove in right behind him. I couldn't help him now if he had a problem; I wouldn't even be able to see him. But I'd done this so many times that I trusted the water to torpedo him safely through the mouth of the lagoon and spit him gently back to the surface in a few seconds.

I relaxed and enjoyed my own short thrill-ride and, when my head broke the surface, Draggin was already laughing. I squinted around in the dim light until I saw their heads bobbing in front of me. Suddenly cold, I took a few strokes to catch up with Draggin. Where the current slowed, we stood up and hurried after Cat, who was already scrambling toward shore. We climbed out of the water, stamping our feet for warmth.

"Want to go again?" I asked Draggin through chatter-ing teeth.

Draggin looked back at the rock.

"Nope," he said. "That was perfect. Besides it's freezing." He looked around. "Where did we leave the towels?"

Cat started walking toward the rock where we'd left our things, with Draggin and me close behind her. Draggin was right—it felt like the temperature had dropped twenty degrees. I glanced at the partially covered moon. How could a bit of cloud make that much difference? I looked around, senses suddenly alert. Something was different, but I couldn't quite put my finger on it.

A huge shiver rattled down my spine—and it wasn't just the cold.

# CHAPTER 4
# MALILA

Cat looked around the rock, then turned and poked Draggin in the chest. *Where'd you put our things?* she signed.

Draggin began searching in wider circles around the rock. "My hearing aids . . . did anyone bring a flashlight?" he asked.

"Sure, it's right here in my bag, Stupid," Cat said.

Cat and I were cold and annoyed, but Draggin looked really upset. He stopped searching around the rocks and looked up and down the beach. "Hey, is that someone sitting there by the trees?" he asked. In the semidarkness we couldn't tell if it was a rock, a bush, or a person against the tree. Draggin walked toward the form. I scrambled after him with Cat trailing me.

Draggin stopped a couple of metres away from an older woman leaning against a big fir. "Uh, hi," he said.

She nodded slightly, and he continued through chattering teeth. "Did you see anyone else on the beach while we were in the water? We left our clothes over there and now they're gone." He stood shivering and pointing toward the scene of the crime.

When the woman spoke, Draggin moved forward to see her face more clearly.

"I saw where you came to, but I didn't see where you came from," she said slowly. She had a blanket pulled tightly around her, and a single, thick braid lay over one shoulder. Her soft-looking moccasins went half way up her calves. They looked so warm.

Draggin hesitated. "We came from . . . here. We left our stuff right over there before we went in the water. Didn't you see us? Or did you just get here?"

"Been here a while in the quiet, and then I heard laughing and talking, and you came out of the water."

Cat and I stood behind Draggin and listened. He turned to us. "She didn't see anyone." His eyes opened wide, and he turned his back so that the woman couldn't see his hands signing to Cat. *Crazy.*

"Well, we'll keep looking then," Cat smiled at the woman. "Thanks, anyway."

We turned and headed farther up the beach, frantically rubbing our arms and hugging ourselves for warmth as we looked behind rocks and bushes. Finally, Draggin got Cat's attention and signed again. *She must have seen something. Or else she has our stuff.*

Her lips blue with cold, Cat returned to the woman, but before she could say a word, the lady held up her hand like a stop sign. She rose slowly to her feet, took the blanket off her shoulders, and wrapped it around Cat. She motioned to Draggin and me to come and gently shoved us into the warm blanket, too. I was too grateful for the warmth to protest being smushed against the others. The woman watched us curiously.

Cat asked again if she'd seen anyone else.

The woman chuckled quietly. "I didn't even see you. Why are you swimming in December?"

We looked at each other. "Did you say—December?" I asked.

She nodded, and another eerie shiver rippled up the back of my neck. What did she mean? She didn't seem crazy. But I didn't know how to explain the cold—it *felt* like December.

Then it came to me: I was dreaming.

I have great dreams. They're full of action and danger, and surprisingly often, they start in water—usually a swimming pool with a secret door that leads me off to some awesome adventure. The lagoon twist was new, but I could work with that. The best part of my dreams is that nothing bad ever happens. As soon as it gets the least bit scary, I tell myself not to worry because it's only a dream. Of course, most times, as soon as I say it's a dream, I wake up, but at least nothing horrible ever happens. Once, a guy with a gun chased me, but I turned around and yelled at him, "Go ahead and shoot me! It's only a dream!"

But I wanted to see what would happen next on the beach, so I tried not to think of the d-word. I grinned at Cat, but she didn't appear to be enjoying my dream at all.

She glared at me. "What are you grinning about? What's going on here?"

Draggin swung his head toward Cat. "What happened? Why is it so cold and where's our stuff?"

Apparently, no one liked my dream except me. And possibly the lady. She looked pretty relaxed. I watched her carefully to see if she would turn into something else. Like a leprechaun. Or a tiger. No, not a tiger—that might be scary.

"Ouch!" I said. Cat had dug her elbow into my ribs.

"What's wrong with you?" she hissed. "Why are you staring at her like that? Do you know something we don't?"

"Relax, Cat, we're dreaming. Now, shush, let's see what happens . . . OUCH! What the heck?"

"Did you feel that pinch, Genius? Still think you're sleeping?" Cat looked super mad, which meant she felt super scared. My stomach dropped. I shut my eyes tight and screamed silently in my head to wake up. When I opened my eyes, I was still on the beach, in a blanket with the twins, talking to a lady who thought it was December.

I could see the spit, the rock, and the lagoon. I turned the other way. The dock stuck out of the water in its usual place.

Then I did a second take and my heart stopped.

The dock!

Only four old fishing boats sat tied to it, as opposed to the dozen or so sailboats that had been there a few minutes ago. I turned toward the lagoon and looked more carefully this time. There should have been at least six cabins visible from here, but there were no lights anywhere. My mouth went dry.

"Would you excuse us for a moment?" I asked the lady. Still in the blanket, we shuffled sideways down the beach a few steps.

"What the hell?" Cat whispered fiercely. Apparently she'd noticed the same changes.

"Take it easy. We need to examine the evidence." Draggin was turning into the dreaded Mr. Science. "The dock appears to have fewer boats. Plus it *feels* like December out here. Something's up." He looked at the moon for a second. "World's biggest practical joke?" He shrugged.

I rolled my eyes and turned away from him as best I could, considering that we were trapped together in a blanket. I focused on Cat. "Maybe the moonlight is playing tricks on our eyes. Or maybe the power's out." Both ideas seemed reasonable. I started to calm down a bit.

"And the temperature drop?" asked Cat.

I looked at her. Yes, what about the temperature drop? And the fact that we couldn't find our clothes? How could moonlight change sailboats to fishing boats? I felt the hair stand up on the back of my neck again, and then suddenly, I felt so dizzy I thought I'd throw up. I burst out of the blanket, took a few steps forward, and sucked in big gulps of cold air.

"Are you alright?" Cat's voice sounded strangely calm, considering the situation. She put her hand on my shoulder, and I felt better. I got back into the blanket and chewed a fingernail.

The woman watched us closely.

A weird moan came from Draggin—as if he'd eaten too much candy—and he stepped out of the blanket with his back to the stranger.

*What?* Cat signed.

Draggin signed so fast that his hands blurred. I thought I saw "magic," and then his hands slowed so I could read them. He tapped his wrist twice and made a curved V with the first two fingers of his right hand, then moved it slowly in a semicircle.

"Bunny time? What did he say?" I turned to Cat for the translation as she glared at him with her daggers of anger-fear.

"What?" I asked again.

"He said 'time travel,'" she whispered.

# CHAPTER 5
# TRAVELLING

Draggin signed to Cat, his hands flying close to his chest, while I hung on to the blanket.

"Slow down," I whispered. "All I understood was 'museum.'"

Draggin's hands fell silent, but he looked at the woman with concern. He pulled us farther down the beach and started to talk. Cat interrupted and told him to lower the volume. Draggin has a hard time hearing himself without his aids, so whispering is definitely not one of his super powers.

"I just remembered a museum display I saw called 'The Legend of Manson's Lagoon.' There were stories from different years about people suddenly appearing in the lagoon. It was like a great mystery that kept coming back, and the stories supposedly go back to a First Nation legend. I didn't read the whole thing, but it was definitely about people popping up out of nowhere into the lagoon—just like us."

"How did you get time travel from that?" I asked.

"Well, if the stories were true, what else would it be?" he said.

"I'm lost. You heard some stories about people popping out of the lagoon a zillion years ago, and therefore we've time-travelled? Bit of a stretch, dontcha think?"

"It's twenty degrees colder, the cabin lights are gone, the sailboats are gone—we dove down in our time, we came up in another."

"But look around you. If we were in the future—or the past—wouldn't *everything* be different?" I dragged us farther up the beach toward the dock. I pointed to the parking lot where there had been at least a couple of cars when we'd walked past.

There were no cars.

Beyond that sat a building where there shouldn't have been one.

"I . . . I . . ."

Draggin followed my gaze and grinned. "The museum! Maybe they still have that display!"

Cat smacked the back of Draggin's head. "You dolt. That's not the museum. It's the old store, before it got dragged up to Beasley Road to become the museum."

"Oh, right," said Draggin, rubbing his head. "What year did they do that?"

"Who knows? But we're obviously in the past."

I threw up my hands. "Stop it! My head is going to explode."

"Well, let's hear your theory then, Maddy," said Cat. "And don't say we're dreaming or I'll pinch you again."

I sighed. "I don't have a theory. Well, except that I'm losing my mind." Their theory seemed better. "What now?" I asked, my teeth chattering so hard I couldn't even bite my nail.

"I say we go talk to the old lady and see what she knows," said Draggin in his not-so-whispery whisper.

*Quiet!* Cat spelled it out quickly, keeping her hand hidden from the woman's view.

As we shuffled back up the beach, I thought about Draggin's theory and I felt dizzy and sick again. We stopped our crab walk in front of the woman who sat against the tree as before. No one wanted to leave the warmth of the blanket. I poked Draggin, who poked Cat.

"I'm Cat, and this is Maddy, and that's Draggin," Cat said from inside our soggy-kid burrito.

The woman nodded but said nothing. We waited. Still nothing. Finally I blurted, "What's your name?"

"My name is Malila."

Cat's right hand spelled it quickly for Draggin.

I poked Draggin again. Draggin poked Cat. "Well, it's nice to meet you, Malila," she said. "And thank you for the use of your blanket. We were wondering if you could help us."

Malila finally spoke. "We'll go to my home and get you warm. I have some clothes that should fit, and you can sleep. We'll find your things tomorrow."

Have you ever had a moment where you had no idea how much you needed something until you got it? Like a glass of water when you didn't know you were thirsty? Or hearing the dentist say, "No cavities"? When Malila said we could go to her house, my shoulders loosened and my stomach unclenched. I'll tell you this about scary, dimension-warping adventures: You don't want to face them in a bathing suit and water shoes.

The twins must have felt the same way because no one mentioned the fact that we were going home with a complete stranger. When Malila got up and walked off the spit, we followed.

The trail to Malila's house took us off the beach and into the woods. As soon as I breathed in the earthy scent, I felt calmer. I could almost believe everything was back to normal as we walked through the familiar cedars.

The uphill trek warmed us up a bit. We took turns with the blanket and moved quickly behind Malila, who negotiated the trail with the light from the moon as it splintered through the treetops.

Soon, we walked across a small clearing and then around a huge garden to a welcoming cabin with smoke wafting from the chimney. Malila unlatched the heavy wooden door and pushed it inward. The warmth of the fire greeted us, and we nearly wedged ourselves in the doorway as we rushed inside.

Draggin closed the door and the comforting glow of a kerosene lantern filled the one room, which served as living room, kitchen, dining room, and bedroom. The cabin's rough wooden walls and floor, the heavy furniture, the murky windows, and the soft light reminded me of pictures of the pioneer homes displayed in the Cortes museum.

"Sit." Malila set the lantern on a small counter and rummaged through a cedar chest at the foot of her iron-framed bed. We looked around the room for seating options. There was a rocker by the fire, and two benches, one on either side of the table. Draggin and I pulled one of them closer to the stove, and we huddled on it together. It felt so good to get warm again.

Malila dropped an armload of clothes on the floor in front of us and said, "Better get outta that wet underwear." Everyone blushed, but no one wanted to explain our bathing suits.

A sheet hung over a thin rope strung from one wall to the other. Malila pulled it closed, separating her bed from the rest of the cabin.

We selected garments from the pile she'd dumped in front of us. The choices were limited. Since our bathing suits were nearly dry from the fire, we left them on and put Malila's clothes over top. The thought of getting naked in another dimension was too weird.

I ended up with a black and red plaid button-up shirt, with sleeves that stopped well short of my wrists, and denim overalls. Cat got brown corduroy overalls and a heavy cotton shirt, green. Draggin found a pair of jeans that fit and a plaid shirt, brown and black. We took off our water shoes and placed them in front of the fire to finish drying, and then we pulled on the deliciously warm wool socks we found in the pile.

Malila put a tin plate of thickly sliced bread and a jar of jam on the table. She watched us tug at the clothes awkwardly. "Sorry girls—I only have grandsons. Small ones. Come eat."

"Where do your grandsons live?" I asked.

"Away," she said softly and turned back to the sink.

While we ate, Malila spread blankets on the floor in front of the wood stove and layered a cozy bed. She stirred the embers and added a log to the fire.

The bed looked inviting. I crawled close to the stove, and Cat and Draggin lay down beside me. Malila put another blanket over us.

I was tired, but I knew I'd lie for hours trying to figure out what had happened.

The fire snapped and hissed as Malila moved about behind the curtain. The glow of the woodstove danced across the dark screen of my closed eyes, and I was surprised at how relaxed I felt. Perhaps I would be able to sleep after all.

# CHAPTER 6

# HUCKLEBERRY SURPRISE

In the morning I woke with a jolt. I nudged Cat, reached across her, and punched Draggin. "Wake up you guys—I know how to get back."

Draggin sat up immediately. Cat yawned, stretched, and punched Draggin too, for no particular reason. She turned to face me. "How?"

"The mouth of the lagoon. It must be some kind of gateway. I don't know why I didn't think of it last night. We go through again and we'll be back in our own time."

"Does have a certain logic to it," said Draggin. "So we wait around until the lagoon fills and do it again?"

I nodded.

"What do we say to Malila? Or should we just sneak away?" Cat signed her questions to Draggin as she whispered them to me.

We turned to see Malila pick up a bucket and head outside. When the door closed, Draggin spoke.

"I think we should find out what year it is, but without letting her know about us."

"How are we gonna do that?" asked Cat.

I got up and looked out the window. Malila pumped water into a bucket. What would happen to us if we said we were from the future?

"Let's tell her we think some of our friends must have stolen our clothes, and we're gonna go find them. Then we'll sneak back to the lagoon and wait for the high tide," said Cat.

"So how do we find out what year this is?" Draggin asked.

"What difference does it make? No one's ever going to believe us anyway," said Cat.

I watched her comb her fingers through her hair. If I tried that on my frizzy mess, I'd probably never get my hand out.

Draggin stared at his sister. "Are you nuts? How can you not want to know what year it is?" I turned back to the window while they nattered at each other. Malila approached the cabin with the water, so I went out to carry the bucket the rest of the way for her.

"Thank you . . ."

"Maddy," I said.

"Maddy. And tell me the other names again? Such strange names."

"Cat and Draggin. Those are nicknames, though. She's actually Alicia—it's a long story. And his name is Duncan. And that's an even longer story, now that I think about it. My name is short for Madison."

"Madison. What does it mean?"

As far as I knew, it didn't mean anything. Maybe an avenue in New York, but that was about it. For a second, I thought about making something up—goddess of lightning, perhaps. "Nothing," I said and shrugged. "What does yours mean?"

"Salmon swimming quickly up a rippling brook," she said.

I looked at her to see if she was joking, but she wasn't. Now my name really seemed boring.

"How did you kids get here?" she asked.

My face went red. Malila held open the cabin door, and I walked through slowly to buy myself time to think of an answer. Obviously, she thought that our arrival was strange—and definitely more than kids stealing each other's clothes.

"How did we get here?" I repeated her question loudly, hoping one of the twins would rescue me. Both heads swivelled in my direction, but no one spoke.

"Well," I started slowly. "We decided to go lagoon-diving at night, to see what it would be like." I looked at the twins over Malila's shoulder. They signed frantically to each other.

I continued. "And so we dove in, and when we came up, our clothes were gone."

My eyes shifted between Malila and Cat. I am not a particularly gifted liar, largely due to my insta-blush face.

A crossroad approached in my story. Should I lie? Or tell the truth? My palms were sweaty.

Behind Malila, Cat signed at me. I frowned at her; I didn't know the sign she kept flashing. So she spelled it: *T-R-U-T-H.* Her face didn't match what she was spelling, so I hesitated. Had I missed something? I could feel time whooshing by as Malila stared at me. I made a desperate decision.

"When we jumped in, it was August and now it's December," I blurted. "The store is at the landing instead of being a museum, there's no electricity or running water, and the sailboats are gone . . . so what year is this anyway?"

I finally took a breath and looked back at Cat, whose face had gone pale and her eyes huge. Draggin had clapped his hand over his mouth as if he was watching a horror movie.

Apparently, I'd missed the "don't tell her" part of Cat's message.

Malila didn't look surprised, though, so I thought she hadn't heard me. But she had.

"It's 1941," said Malila.

I listened to my heart tick like a second hand through a very long minute. Malila told us to come sit by the fire but didn't say anything. Cat and Draggin appeared to be searching for house flies on the ceiling, so I cleared my throat and asked Malila what she thought of my story.

"It is a powerful story. Reminds me of one I heard many times as a little girl."

All three of us leaned forward. "Could you tell us the story, please?" I asked. "Maybe it will help us figure out what happened."

She nodded and settled into her rocker while we got comfortable on the floor.

"It is the story of the Messenger," she said. "Long before the white man—or any others—came to this island, my people believed that when the Creator breathed into the water and made it sparkle, it could heal sickness or injury. The people swam in the spirit water to keep themselves healthy."

*That's the bioluminescence she's talking about,* Draggin signed to Cat.

*Don't ruin the story, Jerk,* Cat signed back.

"They considered the lagoon a special place, full of power. Every summer, at the highest tide, the people would gather by the lagoon at the full moon to honour the ocean that fed them. On one of these occasions, a man rose up out of the lagoon as if from nowhere. He gave the people even more to be grateful for. He showed them secret coves where there were many crabs, showed them a hidden river mouth where the salmon ran like a red road, showed them hidden patches of mushrooms and great ridges of huckleberry bushes. He showed them where to find the softest nettles, the fattest clams, and the juiciest berries. Then he dove from the rock into the lagoon, and they never saw him again. And every year, the people gathered at the highest tide to see if the full moon might bring another messenger from the Creator."

I closed my gaping mouth and nudged Draggin, whose mouth also hung open. "Have there ever been any other messengers since that first one?"

"There were stories from time to time."

"Do people still do that? Go to the lagoon to watch for messengers?" Cat asked.

"Not so much anymore, but sometimes one or two may go." Her dark eyes twinkled. That's why she'd been sitting alone so late at night. "Now I have a question," she said.

Here it comes, I thought. Now we'll know whether she thinks we're crazy or messengers from the Creator.

"Where did you learn the hand-talking?" She lifted her chin slightly in the direction of the twins.

Cat and Draggin looked at each other, and then Cat explained Draggin's hearing to Malila. She seemed delighted with the various ways he could communicate and silently mouthed random phrases to see if he could lip-read them. He could do it, of course, but she chuckled every time like it was a magic trick.

"Why is your wristwatch so big?" she asked him. Draggin showed her his waterproof watch, which also made her laugh.

"Malila?" I drew her attention away from Draggin's arm. "You don't seem too surprised about us being from the future. You believe us?"

Malila tilted her head. "I *was* surprised when I saw three heads appear out of nowhere. But magic lives in the lagoon and also in the stories. So I think you have a message for me." She sat back in the chair and rocked gently.

I really hated to disappoint her. "I'm sorry, Malila. We aren't messengers. We're just kids who accidentally went through some kind of time portal." She stared at the fire, and I couldn't tell if she was disappointed or not.

"We need to get back to our own time," I said. "We're going to dive again at the next high tide."

She kept rocking. "So, you will return to the water and see what happens. But now, you must eat." And with that, she pushed herself up out of the rocker and started making breakfast.

After we ate and helped Malila with the chores, we explored the cabin and tried to keep Draggin from turning every new discovery into a boring history lesson. Cat punched him when he went on for too long about the "current alternatives to refrigerators."

"Ouch!" He rubbed his shoulder and glared at both of us. "Well, do *you* know how to keep milk and butter fresh without a fridge?" he snapped.

"Shut up, Draggin!" Cat and I chorused, and he stomped outside to examine the water pump.

My mom always says that living on Cortes is like living a few decades behind the rest of the world, so some things about 1941 felt familiar. In 2015, old outhouses stood in many yards, and some homes still had no indoor toilet. Most were heated with wood stoves. But pretty much everyone had electricity. Of course, we had a lot of power outages, too, with many trees to fall on the lines during storms. Malila's house reminded me of a rustic cabin after the power had been out for a few days.

But those cabins always felt cluttered—every spare inch covered by stuff, and things in which to keep stuff and extra emergency stuff. This little home appeared neat and tidy, and everything seemed to have a use. I thought of my own bedroom, with its shelves full of dust-covered junk I hadn't used in months or even years. Malila's place had no dust.

In one corner a canoe paddle leaned against the wall, propped up on its handle. The blade had a beautiful carving on it. It took me a minute with my head turned sideways to recognize the black and red Orca. "This is so neat. Where did you get it?" I asked Malila.

"Payment for a baby," she replied.

"Excuse me?"

She laughed at the look on my face. "I'm a midwife. A family gave me that paddle after the arrival of their child. Came in the middle of a storm. His was a good birth. Strong."

I ran my fingers over the smooth grooves of the paddle and imagined how it would feel in my hands, pulling against the water.

"What does the word *midwife* mean?" I asked. I'd always wondered where the word came from.

"Don't know. The word in my language means *to watch—to care.*"

"I like that," I said, then hesitated.

I should be saying more, asking more. But somewhere inside me, I felt as if I already knew Malila. Her kindness and patience seemed . . . familiar. "Thanks, Malila. For everything."

She smiled right into the part of me that knew her.

"I think I'll go outside and explore a little."

She nodded and stoked the fire.

Trees and salal had been cut back to make a clearing. A large garden plot sat in the middle, surrounded by a droopy rope fence that looked like fish nets. Moss, short shrubs, and weeds covered the uneven ground outside the garden. As I walked across the clearing, I noticed movement near the trees and watched a doe and two fawns walk quietly into the woods. Malila had the same lawn mower that many Cortes homes still used in my time— the deer.

I explored the small, three-walled woodshed with its chopping block and neatly organized stacks of rounds, split wood, and kindling. I was in charge of firewood at my house, so I could appreciate Malila's tidy woodshed.

As the morning wore on, I started to get jumpy. When the twins started to snipe at each other, I waded in as referee, happy for a distraction from the questions that filled my head like the water fills the lagoon: *Is the slipstream the portal? Is the second tide strong enough to push us through time? Will we get back to our own world?*

At eleven thirty we headed back to the beach with Malila trailing behind, carrying her basket, and humming. She looked as if she was out to enjoy a sunny picnic.

The lagoon was filling quickly. We said goodbye to Malila, thanking her for her help. Then we counted to three and ripped off our clothes. In the same order as before, we swam out to the rock where we sat pressed against each other for warmth in our ridiculously thin bathing suits.

I waved to Malila across the water. She sat under the same tree as last night, eating dried huckleberries.

"Okay, that looks like the fastest the current is going to get." I stood up and helped the other two to their feet. "Let's go one right after the other so, no matter what happens, we don't get separated. Who wants to go first?"

"I will," Cat said through chattering teeth. She quickly made sure Draggin and I were ready and dove in. As soon as her feet disappeared, Draggin dove, and right after him, I went. As I flew through the slipstream, it suddenly occurred to me that maybe the gate went only one way. What if getting back required drifting out of the lagoon mouth as it drained into the ocean? Maybe we were pushing through the entrance again and going some-where else. Or some*when* else.

When my head broke the surface, I twisted my shoulders around in the water until I spotted one head, then two. But the water was still frigid. And when I turned to face the shore, my heart sank to see Malila waving cheerfully, still munching on berries.

# CHAPTER 7

# HISTORY CHANNEL

Back in our borrowed clothes and huddled once again in front of the warm fire, we endured a long, disappointed silence before Draggin opened the discussion. "Well, that didn't work," he said, and Cat smacked him.

Were the twins shaky and nauseated, too? Maybe not. As much as they fought, they were connected, and I suddenly wished I had a brother to be marooned in time with.

Behind us, Malila sliced bread for our lunch. I gnawed a fingernail in the meantime.

"So, are we stuck here forever or what?" I asked the twins.

"No!" Cat said. "We need to figure this out. We know we time travelled and that it happened in the mouth of the lagoon. Down in 2015, up in 1941. Agreed?"

Draggin and I nodded, and she continued. "And according to the history of the lagoon, we are not the only people who have done this. There seems to be a gate or portal, right?"

"Right," I said, grateful for Cat's logical mind. My stomach started to settle down.

"Because of Malila's legend, we're guessing that the portal is open for the full moon, but that might be a coincidence."

"Hey!" Draggin bolted upright. "The story at the museum had a full moon, too. I forgot. Every one of those mysterious things happened at the full moon. Tomorrow's the full moon—we'll be able to get back tomorrow!" Then his excited face clouded over. "But we came two nights *before* the full moon."

So what did that mean? I glared down at my hands as though they might tell me the answer.

Cat turned away from the fire. "Malila, did the original messenger come and go in the same day?"

Malila put down the knife and turned to us. "They went to many different spots far away from each other and from the lagoon. Would have walked a long way. Must have been at least a couple of days. Unless they used magic."

Cat turned back to us and continued: "Okay, the original visitor stayed a few days, which means the portal remains open for a while, several days perhaps, around the full moon."

"Then why didn't we get through?" I rubbed my aching stomach.

"Maybe it isn't the full moon here," said Draggin. "Malila, when's the full moon? What is the date, anyhow?"

"Almost full tonight. December twenty-second," she said, placing the food on the table.

"Did the messenger dive on the incoming tide both times?" Cat asked Malila.

"Don't know." Then Malila added brightly, "Have you thought of my message yet?"

My fear instantly turned into frustration. "There is no message!"

Malila brushed my anger aside with a soft chuckle. "I think you came here to tell us something no one here can know, and I don't think that gate is going to open for you until you figure it out."

My heart thudded.

"What if she's right?" I said. "It would explain why we didn't get through when our information says we should've."

"Information? It's not exactly a scientific process we're using here! We're guessing and hoping, mostly." Draggin puffed the hair out of his eyes.

"Shut up, Draggin," Cat and I hissed in unison.

"Come. Eat," said Malila.

We picked at the lunch she'd made, each of us lost in our own thoughts. I tried to think of a message we might have been "sent" with. And what did that mean, anyway? Sent by whom? I shivered and took a sip of tea.

"Maybe we're supposed to warn them about pollution and environmental damage," said Draggin.

"Clear-cutting the forest," I said.

"Overfishing," Cat added.

"Or not to buy iPhones until at least iPhone 5!"

"Shut up, Draggin!" Cat couldn't reach him, so I slugged his shoulder.

"Thank you," she said.

"You are most welcome."

Malila munched away contentedly, watching us. "I guess you'll be here a while. I'll go catch a fish for supper. You want to come?"

*Fish. Supper.* My brain attached itself to these simple ideas gratefully and left behind the ones that were giving me a headache: *Message. Time travel.* I needed to try to pay attention to the present and forget about the future. Or should I say, pay attention to the past, which was currently our present.

"I'll come," I said. "Where are we going?"

"To the dock. Then if we don't catch one, maybe we buy one." She got up and started clearing the table.

I jumped up to help, but she sent me out to the shed to get her fishing pole instead. Cat and Draggin came with me.

"Going fishing? Seriously?" Cat looked mad again.

"It's okay, Cat. I'm starting to feel like things are going to work out somehow. We need to relax and keep our eyes and ears open." I could feel myself blushing. "I know I freaked out, but this message thing feels right to me. We're trying too hard. So, yeah, let's go fishing!"

"Whoa! Maybe this is the message," said Draggin, pointing into the shed. He puffed out his chest and spoke deeply. "Malila, we have travelled through time to tell you to upgrade your fishing rod." He laughed. "Look at that thing; it must be at least fifty years old!" Then he grinned sheepishly. "Oh, right."

I've never really liked fishing, so as soon as we got to the dock and Malila started casting, the twins and I wandered off to look at the boats tied up alongside. We walked down the ramp connecting the wharf to the lower, floating dock.

At the far end, three men stood talking; the first in a uniform, the second in a suit, and the third—the only one who looked like he belonged—in galoshes and wool. He gestured at a boat with his pipe. I could smell the tobacco.

I grabbed Cat's elbow and pulled her to a stop. "What do we say if they talk to us?" I whispered.

"That we're visiting Malila. From Vancouver." She signed this to Draggin.

The scene looked odd to me. A uniform or a suit on the dock would be weird in our time, but it probably seemed much stranger in 1941. "Can Draggin see what they're saying?"

Cat nudged Draggin and signed quickly. He faced the trio of men, while Cat and I pretended to study a bowline knot.

"Those other two are police—RCMP—and they're trying to find a particular boat. The fisherman says the white one on the end is the one they're looking for. Whoa!"

"What?"

"I think he called it a 'Jap boat'!" said Draggin.

As the fisherman clomped past us, we froze. He looked us over and frowned.

The policemen dragged a heavy chain onto the dock from a small motorboat. They chained the freshly painted white troller to the dock and secured it with a heavy-duty padlock. Malila walked up behind us. "What happened?"

"Those guys are police and they locked up that boat. The other guy pointed it out to them and he called it a 'Jap boat,'" I said quietly.

Malila watched the scene at the end of the dock carefully. One of the men nailed something to the cabin door, and then they both climbed into the motor boat and putted away.

Malila brushed by us. "That's Mr. Tagawa's boat," she said.

We followed her down the dock and watched as she carefully examined the chain and padlock. Time travel didn't worry her, but this did?

"What's going on, Malila?" I asked. "Should we go see what they nailed to the door?"

Malila nodded, and Draggin and I stepped aboard. We found a typed letter with the Royal Canadian Mounted Police crest at the top of the page. I started reading, but I spluttered to a stop after a string of unfamiliar words. Draggin kept reading, though. He finished and stared across the water at nothing.

"What?" Cat asked from the dock.

I nudged Draggin. "What?" I asked when he looked at me.

"The government has impounded the boat. The letter is signed by the Security Commission." He looked at Cat, then me. "Don't you get it? This is December 22, 1941!"

"So?" Cat asked.

"What exactly do you do during Social Studies class? We just studied this last year. World War Two! Pearl Harbour! Japan attacked the United States less than two weeks ago, and this is the beginning of the internment. They impounded Japanese fishing boats right after Pearl Harbour." He looked excited.

I looked at Cat and could see the wheels turning in her mind. Her right eyebrow shot up. "The internment— of course!"

"What does internment mean again?" I asked. The word sounded familiar, but I couldn't remember what it meant.

"It was when Japanese Canadians were forced to move east," said Cat.

"Oh, right." It was coming back to me. We'd studied it in school, too. I looked at Draggin's flushed face. "Bet you've read all about it," I said.

"I did a huge research project on it. This is like the History Channel, only real. This is so cool." He started walking down the dock, then stopped. He turned to find us staring at him: Malila with her usual curiosity, and Cat and I with disgust.

"What?" he asked looking back and forth between us. "What?"

"Cool?" said Cat, glaring at him. "People lost their homes, businesses, boats . . . families were separated . . . children were sent to prison camps! Which part do you think is 'cool'?"

At these last words, Malila's face clouded over. "Prison? Why would children go to prison?"

"Because they're Japanese!" Cat spit out.

Malila looked at Cat and Draggin again. "Are you Japanese?" she asked.

"No, we're Chinese." I could tell Cat wanted to say something about *that* part of Canadian history as well, but she bit her lip. "But whoever owns this boat is most likely going to prison camp. Soon."

"Mr. Tagawa is going to a prison camp? How do you know?" Malila asked.

"Because we studied it in history class. Your present is our past, remember? This really happened. Or happens. Or is about to happen," I answered.

Studying my face, Malila tapped her fingertips together lightly. The silence stretched on, and my mind spun with images from our class. I remembered a picture of the Bon Odori festival at an internment camp: all those beautiful, bright kimonos; a line of dancing girls; and behind them, the grey barracks of a prison camp. I shuddered.

"Come. We'll go talk to Mr. Tagawa and tell him about his boat," said Malila. "You tell me more about the prison camp."

I waited until Malila had started walking, then grabbed Cat and Draggin. "Should we be telling her this stuff? What if it's like *Back to the Future* and we're screwing up the space-time continuum or something?"

Draggin frowned and Cat laughed. "Get a grip, Maddy. That's just an old movie. Oh, look over there—is that a 'flux capacitor'?" She laughed again and started walking. Draggin hurried to catch up with Malila and begin his history lesson. Or, for her, a current events lesson.

"So, did you hear about the Japanese air force attacking the American naval base in Hawaii a couple of weeks ago?" he asked Malila.

"Yes."

"Okay. Well, the attack on Pearl Harbour is used as an excuse by some people in our province who don't like the Japanese, and they are going to pressure the government until it agrees to move the Japanese Canadians away from the coast. They'll say it's because they're afraid of a Japanese attack and that there might be spies here to help. They'll say it's for the safety of the Japanese Canadians . . . Well, they'll say a lot of crap, but here's what happens; every single Japanese Canadian who lives along the coast is going to be forced to move east, mostly into camps. The government is going to take their homes and boats and possessions and say they'll take care of it for them until after the war. But they don't. They sell it for cheap and use the money to pay for the camps." He stood quietly for a second, then blew the hair out of his eyes. "I suppose you have no way of knowing if I'm telling you the truth or not."

Malila stopped walking and placed her hands on Draggin's shoulders. Worry rippled the calm surface of her dark eyes. "I believe you. The Creator sent you. Why would you lie?"

As we walked, she asked questions, and Draggin answered them as best he could. He knew so much more about it than I did. Of course, he knew more about everything than most people did. Brain like a sponge, that guy.

I listened carefully, remembering the lessons from school and learning some new things, too.

At Malila's cabin, we warmed up while she packed a bag with some dried apple, salal berry cakes, and a big jar of drinking water. Then we headed through the woods toward the road and began the long trek to Blue Jay Lake.

Before we had gone far, a boy about eight or nine years old came bolting out of the trees onto the road and called to Malila to wait. When he saw the rest of us, he froze and stared like we each had two heads. Apparently, visitors were rare in 1941. Malila went to him, and they spoke briefly. After one last look at the three of us, the boy darted back into the trees and disappeared.

"A baby is on the way. I have to go," Malila explained.

I nodded and turned back toward her cabin. "No, you go," she said. "You know where Blue Jay Lake is?"

"Yes, but . . ."

"Then you go." She told us the way to the Tagawa farm, and I recognized the land she described, but she didn't really mean to send us off without her, did she? In 1941?

"But, what will we say? They don't know us. How will we explain who we are or how we got here or . . ." My nervous, shallow breathing wasn't getting enough oxygen to my brain.

Malila took my hand in hers. "This is the message," she said solemnly. "It isn't for me; it's for the Tagawas. Maybe you know something that could help them. You go to them. It's a long walk. On the way, you'll think about what to say." She touched each of us on the head lightly.

Before I could utter another protest, she was gone. I turned to the twins and prepared for the double barrage, but neither of them said a word. We stared at each other for a few moments. Did they feel what I did: a strange pull toward Blue Jay Lake?

"Are we going?" I asked.

They looked at each other, activating their twin-psychic weirdness, and both nodded at the same time. I led the way up the road, wondering what came next.

# CHAPTER 8
# NEWT

We agreed that we'd rest when we got to Gorge Harbour Road. I squinted ahead as we walked along the trail beside Gunflint Lake. "Something looks different," I said. I took a few more steps and then gasped, "Where's the road?"

We got to the spot where the T intersection should be, and we stood where the sign would point the way to the ferry dock—in about twenty years. But now, there was no sign, no ferry, no road.

The three of us stared glumly into the thick woods.

"Hello," said a voice behind us. I jumped while Cat turned calmly, and Draggin continued to stare into the woods. Cat nudged him, so he turned, and there in front of us stood a boy with messy brown hair. The knees of his pants were caked with mud, and he looked to be about a year younger than us. His face lit up with a crooked grin. "You visitin'?"

"Um, yeah," Cat said. "We're visiting Malila from . . . Vancouver."

"Oh." He looked behind us for Malila. The story could have used some help, but my mind was buzzing around like a hornet at a picnic.

"Where ya headed?" the boy asked.

A few too many seconds ticked by, and then Cat blurted, "We're going to the Tagawas."

The boy's face lit up. "Oh! Is Mr. Tagawa doing a play?"

I took a deep breath. "Yup, a play."

"I love his shadow puppets. You're lucky to be invited." He grinned at us expectantly, and I got even more tense. Was he hoping for an invitation to whatever he was talking about? I thought we might be cooked, but then Cat gave him her most charming smile and I relaxed.

"So, do you know where Blue Jay Lake is?" she said, with a tilt of her head.

"Sure," the boy said. "It's a long ways—seven or eight miles. What are your names?"

"I'm Cat, this is Maddy, and that's my brother, Draggin. What's your name?"

"Newt."

"Is that short for Newton?"

"It's a nickname. Because I love newts. Well, actually, I got the name when I was helping migrating newts cross the road one day and forgot to go to school, and caused a search party."

The boy held up his hands, and in each one, he held a tiny brown newt. He gently placed them into the ditch, wiped his hand carefully on his shirt, and stuck it out for me to shake.

"Pleased to meet you," he said.

"You too." I liked Newt.

He turned to the twins. "I like your name," he said, shaking Cat's hand. "Is your name really Dragon?" he asked Draggin.

"No, it's a nickname."

"Well, you city folk sure have smooth names. Especially you, Dragon." Draggin stood up a little straighter, and Cat and I rolled our eyes at each other.

Newt continued: "Well, you follow this road until you get to Squirrel Cove and then —"

"Excuse me, Newt," Cat broke in. "But, isn't there a shortcut? A trail through the woods?" The road to Squirrel Cove went all the way to the east side of Cortes before curving back to Blue Jay Lake near the centre of the island. We were probably standing more or less directly south of Blue Jay Lake right now.

Newt chewed his lip. "Well, yup, there's a trail, alright. But I don't think that's a good idea."

"Why not?" asked Cat.

"It cuts through Crazy Bill's land, and that's a bad idea even if he knows you. It's a really bad idea for strangers."

I grew up on stories of hermits and "crazies" on Cortes. They were generally people who preferred to be alone— but they weren't dangerous.

"What's so crazy about Crazy Bill?" I asked.

Newt rubbed his chin, then shrugged. "He's just crazy. My pop says he'd shoot ya as soon as look at ya if he catches you on his land. Better you stick to the road."

"How far is it by the trail?"

"I reckon it's about half as far by trail as by road. More or less." He shrugged again.

The three of us shuffled into a huddle, and Cat signed to Draggin. *Did you get that?*

He nodded. "I vote for the short cut. Eight miles will take hours." He looked at his watch. "It's already after one o'clock. It'll be dark by the time we get there if we go around."

I frowned. "No, it won't."

"It's December, Maddy—it'll be dark by five o'clock."

"Oh yeah, I forgot." I looked at Newt. I trusted him and felt we should listen to him, but I agreed with Draggin; there wasn't time. It would be foolish to be out here without lights after dark. I knew the island, but then again I didn't. Not now. I looked into the forest where the road should be—would be—and made my decision. "Draggin's right. We have to hurry," I said.

"Short cut," Cat agreed.

Newt reluctantly agreed to lead us to the trailhead, but he never stopped trying to change our minds. I kept reassuring him that we'd be quiet and quick, but he just shook his head and sighed. He looked very serious as he said goodbye, shaking each of our hands again. We started down the narrow pathway through the salal, and when I turned back after a few metres, he was still there, watching us.

We walked for nearly two hours, then stopped to rest at a creek. We ate the last of Malila's salal cakes, and then Cat and I stone-stepped into the middle of the brook to refill the water jar.

The sound of the stream kept us from hearing the footsteps that crashed through the bush behind Draggin. In fact, no one heard anything until Draggin let out a startled yelp as a shotgun barrel jabbed him in the back. All three of us set eyes on Crazy Bill at the same moment.

Although short and scrawny, he seemed to take up a lot of space. His feet shuffled back and forth in his muddy rubber boots. Suspenders held up his baggy pants, and he wore a filthy grey wool sweater over an even filthier undershirt. No jacket. His matted orange hair was wild and hung over a craggy face covered in grey stubble and grime. Something that looked like a dead mouse covered his upper lip and hung down over his mouth. Maybe that's why they're called moustaches. His grubbiness didn't bother me, but his eyes made me shiver; they were sky blue but dull—and mean—and they darted around like houseflies trapped under an overturned glass.

"I knew it!" he said. "Everybody thought I was nuts, but here you are—Jap spies on Cortes."

Cat stiffened. "We're Chinese and the word 'Jap' is racist."

I grabbed her sleeve and tugged desperately. "Not really the time, Cat," I whispered.

"Well, we're not Japanese and we're obviously not spies—we're kids," Cat continued indignantly.

"Shut up!" Crazy Bill shouted. "You two get over here with this one."

I grabbed Cat's hand, and we stone-stepped back to Draggin while Crazy Bill pointed the gun at us and muttered to himself.

He nudged Draggin again, and the three of us started walking. I shoved Malila's cloth bag under the bib of my overalls and carried the water jar in my hands. Crazy Bill didn't seem to notice that, but when Cat tried to whisper something to me, he rammed the gun into her back and yelled at her to shut up. He muttered about Jap spies and Pearl Harbour and was soon having a full conversation with himself. "They musta hid their boat. I'll find it later. Almost home."

After a few minutes, we stepped out of the trees into a clearing. The path continued across a large open field of weeds and moss. I looked around, trying to get a fix on our location. The sun hung December-low in the sky to my left. The length of a soccer field separated us from the "yard" where the grass had been worn away to create a large dirt courtyard around a cluster of shacks.

We came to a small woodshed that looked like it might be a goner in the next strong wind. To the right and about forty metres past the woodshed, sat a slightly larger, sturdier cabin. Smoke slithered from the chimney. Behind that stood a weathered outhouse, leaning precariously, and beyond that sat a big mess of a garden, with dead plants sticking out of the ground like tombstones.

Crazy Bill stopped us at the first shack. Inside the woodshed, he forced Cat and me to sit back to back on the floor in a layer of dust, cobwebs, and wood chips. Then he bound our hands together with a hard, scratchy rope that bit into my bare wrists. Roughly, he tied my ankles together, and I could feel the pinch through Malila's thick wool socks. He tied Cat's feet as well, then stood up straight and stared down at us for a second or two with those scurrying eyes of his. Then, he grabbed Draggin by the ear and pulled him out the door, bolting it behind him.

"Are you okay?" I asked Cat.

"I'm okay. We have to see where he's taking Draggin. Can we inch our way over to that crack between the boards?"

A door slammed while we slowly wiggled our way across the floor. Cat pressed her face up to the crack and reported that she could see the cabin but couldn't tell if they were in there or not. "We have to think of something! We have to get Draggin."

"I know. I'm thinking," I said. It was scary to hear Cat so rattled.

"Wait—the door's opening," she said, her voice tight.

Cat narrated as Crazy Bill stepped out of the cabin, slid the wooden bolt shut and stomped into the woods, talking to himself angrily. He carried the shotgun.

"Hey!" Cat cried. "Draggin's signing at the window. He wants to know if we can see him." She looked around. "The shovel! If we can get it and wave it in front of the window . . ."

We bum-shuffled across the floor of the shed, carefully gripped the shovel in our bound hands, and wiggled back to the window. Straining, we jerked the handle back and forth, then returned to the crack in the wall.

"He saw it!" Cat said. She translated his signing. "He got himself untied, but he's locked in the cabin. Crazy Bill tried to question him because he really thinks Draggin's a spy. Draggin couldn't understand him because of the moustache, so he called Draggin simple-minded and stormed out. Went to look for our boat." She turned to face me. "Draggin's looking for a way out."

Just then, the door of the woodshed flew open. Cat and Draggin had been so busy reading each other's hands, they'd both failed to notice Crazy Bill approaching from the other direction.

"What are they up to?" he growled. He reached down and grabbed the rope between our hands and dragged us back to the middle of the shed, wrenching my shoulders. He looked around. "Now where'd that anchor git to?" He kicked aside some firewood and dragged a heavy chunk of rusted metal across the floor.

After he'd tied our hands to it, he muttered, "That should keep them put." His eyes darted around like he was trying not to look directly into the sun. Finally, he looked at me sideways with his dead blue eyes. "Tomorrow I'll take you to the police on the big island. Put the Japs in jail and you . . ." He poked a leathery finger in my face. "Well, I reckon if whites help spies, they go to jail, too."

I could feel Cat's anger vibrating through her whole body. I closed my eyes and sent her a telepathic message: *Please don't say anything.* The man and his mucky gumboots stomped out the door, and I exhaled.

"Draggin's loose in the cabin. What if he doesn't see Crazy Bill coming?" Cat's voice flattened with fear, but all we could do was wait.

## CHAPTER 9
# THE PLAN

We sat quietly, straining to hear, and unable to move with the weight of the anchor on our arms. I didn't take a full breath until the shed door flew open and Draggin stumbled in, apparently unhurt, with his hands tied in front of him. Crazy Bill pushed him down to the floor and tied his feet to the anchor. He looked down at us the way a fisherman surveys his catch at the end of a good day.

As Crazy Bill turned to leave, still muttering to himself about spies and boats, Draggin said, "Excuse me, sir, but what about our supper?"

Crazy Bill made a barking sound that I took to be a laugh. "Git your own." He opened the door to leave.

Draggin persisted. "When you take us to the police tomorrow, we'll tell them you didn't feed us—there's laws about that you know. You have to feed prisoners of war or you'll be in trouble. You've heard of the Geneva Convention, haven't you?"

Crazy Bill's bushy eyebrows rushed to meet each other, and his mouth hung open. He considered for a moment, then growled, "'Course I heard of it. I ain't stupid. You'll get your supper when I'm good and ready." He stomped out and bolted the door.

I looked at Draggin. "What did you do that for? Now we have to wait until he comes back before we can try to get away. And what the heck is a Geneva Convention?"

"It's a set of rules about war that will be written in about eight years."

I glared at him.

"What?" he said. "The guy thinks we're Japanese spies. How bright can he be? As for the dinner, I wanted to test him and see if he really is planning to take us to the police tomorrow. Besides, if we do get loose, we have a long walk ahead of us and no food or water."

"Can you get your hands free, Draggin?" I asked.

He wiggled silently, concentration freezing his face for several moments. "No, it's way tighter this time. You?"

"No. If either of us moves, it pulls the rope and hurts us both. And makes the knot tighter. Feet?" Squirming and grunting, we twisted our feet about.

"It's no use," I choked. My panic started to rise again.

"Well, let's look at it logically," Draggin said. "First, we can't get loose and we certainly can't escape tied up. So our options are to scream for help when we have no idea if anyone else is around—or to wait for morning and try to get away when he moves us." Then, as an afterthought, he added, "Or wait until he takes us to the police, but then we have to explain what we're doing here. You don't think the police would believe we're Japanese spies do you?"

"Well, they might believe we're Japanese," Cat said with disgust, "but your name has to start with 'crazy' to believe that twelve-year-olds are spies. But what if he doesn't take us to the police? What if one of the many voices in his head wakes him up in the middle of the night and convinces him to take matters into his own hands?"

That grim idea settled in with the dimming light, and the shadows inside the shed became more and more menacing. Clouds gathered against the full moon. What if Crazy Bill decided to torture us for information? Or even to kill us? Who would know? We were in the middle of nowhere, and only Malila and Newt even knew that we existed in this world. My scalp tingled. "I'm freaking out, you guys! We have to get away from this nutter!"

"Well, what are our assets?" Draggin began. Sometimes he clings to logic like it's a rope swing over a snake pit.

Cat snapped to attention, happy for a place to vent her fear-fuelled anger. "Assets? You twit! We're wearing borrowed clothes that don't fit and water sandals instead of proper shoes. We have no food or water, and the sum total of our futuristic technological advantage is your stupid watch."

The next silence lasted for several long minutes.

"That's it, Cat! My watch." Draggin rocked back and forth like he did when he got excited. I stayed quiet, knowing he still had to work out the details but, hallelujah, he had a plan.

He pulled his bound wrists up to his face and began twisting his hands until he could push the buttons on his watch. "Yes!" he exclaimed. "Okay, here's what we'll do: When you hear Crazy Bill coming in the morning, I'll set my alarm to go off when he's walking us down the trail. Just before it goes off, we'll tell him we have a bomb. He won't believe us, but when the watch beeps, it should startle him enough to give us a chance to run. It'll be a sound he's never heard, and he thinks we're spies. We'll each go in different directions, zigzag so he can't shoot us, and use the trees for cover. We can outrun him easily. If we get separated, we all get back to Malila's cabin any way we can. What do you think?"

Cat shuddered. "I think I would like to wake up from Maddy's stupid nightmare now. I can't believe we're making a plan that's about trying not to get shot. Is this the best we can do?"

Before anyone could respond, the door banged open and Crazy Bill loomed in the doorway, looking crazier than ever in the quickly dimming light.

"Here's your prisoner-of-war grub. Can't say you weren't treated fair. I'll be back at sunup. Enjoy your dinner," he sneered, as he slammed a jar of water on the floor beside Draggin. He pulled three shrivelled apples out of his coat pocket and dropped them beside the jar.

Once he left, we spent the next several minutes struggling to eat and drink, with Draggin feeding Cat and me. His hands were tied together, but at least they were in front of him. We moved like a three-headed, two-handed, six-legged monster, nearly spilling the precious water several times. At last we'd each eaten an apple and had a good drink. I spit out the seeds. "I've never eaten that much of an apple before in my life."

I tried to get a bit more comfortable, but in every position I tried, my neck ached from the weight of my arms pulling backwards on my shoulders. Being tied to Cat made it worse. Draggin slid a piece of firewood between our backs so we could rest our hands a few inches off the floor, which helped a lot.

Once the pain subsided, I noticed the cold. None of us were dressed properly for December, and cold air streamed in between the boards of the shed. Cat and I pushed ourselves closer together. Malila's warm blanket popped into my head. "Hey, do you think Malila will get worried and come looking for us?"

"She could be with that baby's family for days," Cat said. "Besides, if she does go home and we're not there, she'll assume we're spending the night at Tagawa's. Or that we delivered our message and went back to the lagoon for the midnight tide."

That thought depressed me even more. What if the next high tide was our last chance to get home, and we sat here, tied up in the woodshed of a crazy hermit? I tried to think of something positive. "Well, maybe Malila will call the Tagawas and check on us."

"Maddy, it's 1941! There's probably one phone on the whole island," said Draggin.

"Oh, ya." I blushed.

"Hang on," Cat said. "Maybe Crazy Bill left his cell phone lying around, and we can text Malila."

My laugh was feeble, but I felt better.

As darkness fell like a heavy curtain, I was thankful I wasn't alone. Pressing my back against Cat did more than warm me; it kept my panic away. I leaned my head lightly against hers.

"So how crazy do you think this guy actually is?" I asked Cat softly.

"Well, he's no fan of the Differents," she replied.

Being a "Different" is a Beaton-family thing. When Draggin's parents found out baby Duncan was hard of hearing, they decided to ensure it had a positive impact on his life. So, as the twins grew up, the family called little Duncan "a Different" and really celebrated it. They told stories of famous Differents. Cat got jealous, so they explained that everyone is a Different in some way and they celebrated her as well. They did a great job with Draggin, though; at the end of the first week of kindergarten, every five-year-old in the class wanted to learn the "hand talking" and get hearing aids of their own.

Cat and I had talked about this before. We both agreed that everyone is a Different in one way or another—and everyone sure feels like one. But Cat got cranky when I suggested that all differences are basically the same. And who am I to argue? I'm a slightly hyperactive redhead; she's Asian in a mostly white country. I guess she should know.

"Well, I think Crazy Bill has more going on than a lack of respect for the Differents. He really creeps me out, Cat. It feels like he could be capable of anything."

"Stop thinking about it. We'll get away from him in the morning. It'll be okay."

I closed my eyes to rest for a moment and drifted off to the dog show I went to last year with Grandpa Paul. I could feel Grandpa's warm hand holding mine, and I felt so happy and safe. I munched on cotton candy and watched the dogs being groomed for the competition. When we stopped to watch a little white Westie, I turned to Grandpa and told him I felt chilly and hungry. Grandpa said he'd go get me something, and he walked away. When I turned back to the dog, his eyes had turned red, and suddenly I was freezing cold. I shivered, and everything went dark. The two red eyes were all I could see.

My head snapped forward, and I woke up. I'd been dreaming, and when I remembered Crazy Bill's woodshed, my stomach dropped sickeningly.

But if the dream was over, why were the eyes still there?

They floated in the darkness about three inches off the floor. I tried to clear the fuzziness from my head. The darkness was disorienting, but the longer I looked, the more certain I became; it was a rat. I wrapped my hand around the piece of wood under our wrists and nudged Cat gently.

"Psst—Cat, wake up. Look over to your right. Do you see the rat?" Cat came awake immediately. I felt her head turn.

"Oh gawd, Maddy. I hate rats. Make it go away, or I'm gonna lose it completely."

"Work with me," I whispered, slowly lifting the piece of wood and preparing to throw it as best I could with my hands tied to Cat's. Just before I tossed it, the rat beeped and disappeared.

"What's up?" Draggin's sleepy voice filled the darkness.

"What was that beep?" I hissed. He couldn't hear me because he couldn't see me.

"It's his watch," Cat said. Draggin rustled about, and then his watch beeped again. He made it glow for a second, and we could see him lying in the spot where I'd seen the "rat."

"I set my alarm for six o'clock, so we'd be awake before he came out here," he said, yawning.

"Good grief, that was close."

"What?"

"We were preparing to kill your wrist. We thought it was a rat," I whisper-shouted.

Between the cold and the thought of rats sharing our quarters, we were now shivering, miserable, and wide awake. Occasionally, we talked about things like the best breakfast we ever had or the softest bed we ever slept in. Cat and I were both stiff and sore from being unable to move much. Draggin could move some, but he had no one for warmth.

"I'm freezing. Can I sit closer to you two?" he asked.

"Come on," Cat said. Draggin got as close to his sister as the anchor would allow, and we went over the fake bomb plan again. Did bombs beep in 1941?

None of us knew.

## CHAPTER 10
# ESCAPE

When first light cracked through the darkness of the shed, it brought a sliver of hope. I still felt cold, hungry, and sore, but everything looks better in the daylight, doesn't it? Somehow, we'd be okay.

We went over our plan again and talked about landmarks for getting back to Malila's in case one of us got lost.

As the light chased the last of the shadows from the corners, the sound of footsteps approached, and my fear returned.

Suddenly, our plan seemed ridiculous and dangerous again. I could barely breathe. Cat stiffened behind me. The bolt on the outside of the door jiggled, stopped, and jiggled again. Then the door opened slowly, and there stood Newt.

"Newt! What are you doing here?" I exclaimed.

"Checking up on you three. I've had a bad feeling ever since we parted yesterday. I told you Crazy Bill was crazy." Newt worked at the knots on Draggin's wrists.

Once free, we huddled around the dirty window to keep an eye on the cabin. A thin wisp of smoke rose from the chimney, but we couldn't see Crazy Bill.

"We go one at a time, get behind the shed quickly so he can't see us, and run straight into the woods. I'll go last," Newt said.

I nodded. "Cat, then Draggin, then me, then Newt. Okay?" The twins nodded.

I showed Newt the crack between the boards, and he pressed his face to the wall as Cat got ready at the door. I jammed the water jar back into the bag that I'd been hiding. It felt good to have something in my hands. Something hard and swingable.

"Now!" Newt said quietly, and I opened the door slowly, willing it to be silent. As soon as she could squeeze through, Cat stepped out and took off around the corner of the shed. Draggin went next, and as he disappeared, Newt exclaimed, "Wait." I froze with the door closed.

"Can you see him?" I asked.

"Yes, he's at the window." We both froze—then Newt exhaled. "Okay. Ready? Now!"

I bolted around the corner, through the clearing, and into the woods. I kept running until I saw Cat and Draggin off to my right, jumping up and down and waving their arms to get my attention without making any noise.

The three of us spread out through the woods within sight of each other, to make sure we intercepted Newt. But he didn't come.

And he didn't come.

Either Crazy Bill watched from the window of the cabin again, or—I didn't want to think about other possibilities.

I stood up from my hiding place and waved my arms like a windmill until I got Cat's attention. She and Draggin joined me, and together we ran back to the edge of the clearing.

Once there, we sat and watched quietly for several minutes. The only movement was smoke drifting from the chimney. Perhaps Newt had gotten past us somehow and was looking for us. Or maybe Crazy Bill had already taken him somewhere.

We could get to the back of the woodshed without being seen, but we didn't know if anyone was in there. Cat and I whispered, trying to decide which of us should go. Draggin has a hard time moving quietly, just like he has a hard time whispering.

Cat looked at my completely out-of-control halo of bright red hair and suggested she might be less visible. "Good idea," I said. "You're smaller."

Cat stepped out and moved like her namesake across the clearing. In a matter of seconds, she stood behind the woodshed looking back at us. She signed quickly and Draggin translated in a loud whisper. "The shed is quiet, but she's going to try to look in the window first. If she gets inside, she'll throw a piece of wood out where we can see it."

Cat disappeared from the back of the shed, and Draggin and I sat, barely breathing. Time is weird, isn't it? Goes way too fast when you're having fun and slows to a crawl when you're in agony. I felt years older by the time a small piece of wood tumbled into view around the front corner of the shed.

"She's in!"

Draggin went next. I counted to fifteen, and then I sprinted to the back of the shed. Crouching as low as possible, I moved along the side to the front corner where I peeked out at Crazy Bill's ugly home. I couldn't see any movement, but the windows were so filthy, I couldn't be sure. I sprinted to the shed door, pushed it open, tossed Malila's bag ahead of me, and dove in. Draggin closed the door quickly behind me, and we both sat recovering for a second. Cat monitored the cabin from the crack in the boards.

"Have you seen anything?" I asked her.

"Yes. Crazy Bill is in there, and he's moving around and waving his arms like he's talking to someone. Of course, that doesn't necessarily mean that Newt is in there with him, since he's so fond of talking to himself." She turned to face us. "Now what?"

"I have a plan," Draggin said loudly.

When I shushed him, he blew his hair out of his eyes and continued at a lower volume. "I'm going to go back into the trees behind us and circle around the clearing until I'm behind his cabin. Then I'll sneak up to a window and see what's going on. Cat will watch from here, and I'll tell her what I see. If Newt is in there, we're gonna need some kind of distraction to keep Crazy Bill busy so I can get inside. You guys need to figure that part out."

With her face still glued to the wall, Cat started signing furiously.

"I *will* be quiet, Cat. Don't worry," Draggin said.

Cat's hands flew again.

"Because I don't want you to, and it's too late now because I'm gone." And with that, Draggin—or should I say, Dragon—bolted out the door.

I looked at Cat and saw her lip tremble slightly before she bit down on it and straightened her shoulders.

I put my arm around her while she stared through the crack in the boards.

"So, how do we create a diversion?" she asked me.

Every idea we came up with put us back in danger. We needed the distraction to be some distance away from any of us, and it had to be something that would hold Crazy Bill's interest for long enough. Desperate for an idea, I grabbed Malila's bag and dumped it out on the floor. The water jar was still intact in spite of me throwing it into the shed. A few dried salal berries had fallen to the bottom of the bag where I also found a small stub of pencil and a penny—a King's head! Then I remembered that all pennies had King George on them in 1941 because he was still the King. I also found a tiny scrap of paper that looked like an old shopping list. I turned the bag inside out and shook it, and one wooden match tumbled onto the floor.

Fire!

"There's a match here, Cat! We can start a fire and then take off. Let's see . . . where?"

Cat spoke without turning. "The corner of the wood-shed. His whole supply of wood going up in flames will get him moving. With only one match, this better be the world's best fire start."

I looked around. "There's lots of shavings and splinters on the floor. And I have a scrap of paper." I began to gather everything tiny and combustible, stuffing it into the bag. "Any sign of Draggin?"

Cat inhaled sharply. "There he is! Right at the corner of the cabin." She watched him sign. "He says . . . there's a window in the side wall. Newt's inside, tied up. Crazy Bill is yelling at him—oh gawd—threatening him with a fire poker! We have to hurry."

"Tell Draggin about the fire!" I said.

"Right," she said and stood up to relay the plan to Draggin. Once seated at the spy crack again, she relayed his message. "When Crazy Bill comes to put out the fire, Draggin will go inside and untie Newt, and they'll run north behind the cabin into the trees. We'll head north as well, and Draggin will do his owl call until we find them." Cat exhaled and turned to look at me. "Okay, we have a fire to set. Don't open the door until I tell you." She pressed her face back to the wall.

In my right hand I held Malila's bag stuffed with as much dry leaves, bark hair, and wood splinters as I could find. In my left I clutched that match like it was the last one on earth.

At Cat's signal I opened the door, closed it behind me, and slipped around the corner, out of sight. I made my way around the back of the shed and then crawled up to the front corner and peeked out cautiously. If I could see the cabin, then Crazy Bill could see the fire. Carefully, I covered a small patch of grass with a bed of wood chips.

I started with the crumpled shopping list. On top of that, I piled layers of bark hair and wood shavings. I was ready to add kindling as the fire caught. *If* it caught. With my pyre ready, I tapped on the wall of the shed and waited as the door opened and shut, and then Cat was behind me.

"Ready," she said.

I took the match with a shaking hand and struck it on the metal zipper of my overalls. The flame sputtered, and I shielded it with my other hand as I lowered it slowly.

The flame flared, then flickered. I held my breath. It glowed again, then spread a bit. I leaned forward and blew gently. Then I added more kindling and gradually began to add the larger pieces. Cat moved away from the wall of the shed and signed to Draggin to get Crazy Bill's attention to his front window as soon as we'd left. We stayed long enough to be sure the fire would take hold, and then we bolted. As I turned the corner of the shed, I saw flames licking at the side of the shack.

We sprinted deep enough into the woods to be well hidden, then turned to watch. I could see Draggin crawling along the ground on his hands and knees and staying tight against the wall so he wouldn't be seen from the window above him. He grabbed a handful of dirt and pebbles and tossed it up at the window, then rolled under the cabin and disappeared. I didn't want to think about what might be under there.

The door of the cabin flew open, and Crazy Bill stormed out with his shotgun. He looked around for a second, then spotted the fire working its way up the side of the woodshed. At the sound of his shouts, Cat and I took off.

We headed north, crashing through the bushes and around stumps and hoping that our detours to avoid fallen trees would not throw us too far off course. I ran until I thought my heart would burst and hollered at Cat to stop. With my hands on my knees, I caught my breath and listened to the forest. Faintly, off in the distance, an owl hooted. I had no idea from which direction the sound had come.

"Draggin!" Cat said, her face brightening. "This way," she said and took off again without hesitating. She stopped occasionally to listen again and adjust our course. After about fifteen minutes, Draggin and Newt appeared ahead of us. I couldn't believe we'd found them. Either Cat has amazing hearing, or something other than her ears led her to her twin.

Cat ran straight to Draggin like she planned to hug him, then stopped short. She glanced at Newt, then signed something to Draggin that made him blush and grin. The twins high-fived, and then Cat punched him in the arm to restore the natural order.

A wave of relief surged through me, washing away any words. Newt spoke first.

"Thank you for coming back for me when you don't even know me."

"Well, you don't know us either and you came back first," I exclaimed. "Did Crazy Bill hurt you?"

"No, I'm alright," Newt said.

We filled each other in on the details of our separate adventures. Newt had been ready to run from the shed when Crazy Bill came out of the cabin and stomped toward the woodshed, leaving him no escape.

I shuddered as I pictured Newt alone, with Crazy Bill and his shotgun coming straight at him.

We told Newt our story, and Cat and I described the diversion. Then Draggin asked how we made a fire with no lighter.

"What's a lighter?" asked Newt.

Draggin explained lighters to Newt as though they were a new thing in Vancouver that hadn't reached the islands yet, which was mostly true. Draggin knew way too much about the construction of a lighter.

I looked around. "So, where are we anyway?" I asked Newt.

"Well, we ran straight north from Crazy Bill's. We're probably almost at the road. Once we find it, we go west till we hit the trail again and head for Blue Jay Lake. We should be okay from there."

"We? Are you coming with us to Tagawa's?" I wavered between relief and worry. How would we explain all of this to him? Cat caught my eye, obviously thinking the same thing.

"If it's okay, I'd like to come." Newt looked down at the ground, and his face reddened slightly. "The Tagawas have a son my age named Yoshi. He hasn't been to school in a while—since we heard about the attack on Pearl Harbour. He's my friend."

I turned my attention to Cat and Draggin, who signed back and forth feverishly in a heated discussion. I stepped in front of them to distract Newt, who politely pretended not to notice. "This way," he said and started into the woods.

# CHAPTER 11
## YEAR TRAVELLERS

As Newt trudged off through the trees, I turned to face the twins. "What?"

"Let's tell him everything," Cat whispered.

"You agree?" I looked at Draggin, who nodded. I was relieved. It seemed like the right thing to do.

We hurried to catch up to him. "So, Newt, you remember those lighters?" I asked.

"Yes?"

"Well, we didn't tell you the truth, exactly."

Newt turned around and grinned at me. "I knew it! Why on earth would you bother pouring fuel into a tiny container and then building a tiny flint for it . . . the whole thing sounded pretty ridiculous, if you don't mind me saying so. You can't improve on a match!"

I tucked that bit of wisdom away for later. "Actually, lighters do exist. But where we come from, they're everywhere. And when they run out of fuel, you throw them away and buy a new one."

Newt's mouth dropped open. "Has everyone in Vancouver gone mad?" he asked.

I was handling this badly. "Let me start over. I'm not from Vancouver. I'm from Cortes. I've lived here most of my life. It's just that I haven't been born yet."

I stopped before I could do any more damage and turned to the twins. "Little help?"

Cat rolled her eyes and stepped past me to face Newt, who now stood staring at us with his eyebrows high on his forehead and his mouth frozen in a tight-lipped grimace.

Cat held out her hands, palms down, and smiled reassuringly. "Don't be scared, Newt. We're not crazy or anything. We're from the future. We dove into Manson's Lagoon in our time and came up here in 1941, and we're not sure how to get back. We think we need to warn the Tagawas about something, and then we'll be able to get home. Possibly. We really aren't sure. I know this is a lot to take in . . ." She frowned. "Maybe you should sit down. You don't look so good."

Newt plopped down heavily in the middle of the path. "It's pretty hard to believe," he whispered.

Draggin stepped forward, crouched down, and pulled up the sleeve of his shirt, revealing his digital watch. Newt leaned forward and studied it closely. "When did they start making these?" he asked softly.

"1972," Draggin said. I couldn't believe he knew that.

Newt remained quiet for a long time but kept his eyes on us, as though searching for more evidence. Finally, he spoke. "You came out of the lagoon?"

"Yes," I said, picturing a black creature roaring out of the water.

"Where did you get those clothes?"

"From Malila."

He nodded. "Are those shoes of yours from the future?"

I had forgotten about our water shoes. "They're for swimming. So you don't hurt your feet on shells or barnacles."

He shook his head. "Well, I'll be." He turned to Draggin. "Do lots of people talk like you in the future?"

Draggin blushed. "I'm hard of hearing and I don't have my hearing aids. It's hard for me to hear how I sound." He looked annoyed.

"I think he meant the signing," I said.

Newt asked me if Draggin could hear him. I explained that he could hear a bit, but mostly he was lip-reading. Newt's eyes grew round again and he turned back to Draggin. He opened his mouth wide and moved his lips in large, exaggerated movements.

"Can you understand me?" he asked.

He grinned hopefully at Draggin, who stared back at him with hard eyes. I nudged Newt gently. "Just talk normal," I said.

Once we got Newt off that subject, he wanted to know if the future had flying cars. Draggin told him yes. Cat punched Draggin and told Newt that there were lots more cars and lots more airplanes, but no flying cars. Fortunately, she did not get into space travel, or we'd have been there for hours.

Newt had more questions: How many people lived on Cortes in our time? *About 1000.* Who would win the 1942

Stanley Cup? *Montreal seemed like a good guess.* Would cars ever replace horses entirely? *Very soon.*

He wanted to know what people ate in the future. I told him that here on Cortes, it wouldn't change that much. Finally, he wanted to know how long the war would last.

"Three more years," I said.

He was silent for a long time. Then, he got up and brushed off his pants. "Well," he said, "we better get going, you future-beings." He grinned weakly.

"We prefer 'time travellers,'" I said, and we headed down the path again.

We walked for nearly an hour before I asked Newt how much farther to our destination. When he said we were just over halfway, I begged for a break. We found a stream where we could refill the water jar and sit for a bit, and then Newt fished around in his pocket until he came up with a squished hunk of bread wrapped in wax paper. After hearing we'd had nothing to eat since last night's apples, he insisted we split the bread between the three of us. It wasn't much, but I was grateful to hush the gnawing in my belly for a while.

My feet hurt in the tight-fitting water shoes. I could feel a blister starting. I took another drink of water, hoping to trick my stomach into feeling full. When Newt asked if we were ready to go, I groaned and got up.

"So, are you going to tell the Tagawas you're year-travellers?" Newt asked as we walked.

"Time travellers," I corrected. "And we have no idea what we're going to tell the Tagawas."

Newt chatted away, asking questions about the future, and I did my best to answer truthfully, but I was exhausted. I was hiking on an empty stomach with no sleep, and just when I couldn't answer any more questions, he announced that we were almost there.

With Newt's help, we prepared our cover story as we walked the last part of the path and stepped out of the trees.

Across the clearing, a boy chopped wood beside a sturdy-looking shed. He looked up almost immediately, seeming to sense our arrival, and stood watching us approach.

When we got within earshot, Newt raised his hand in greeting and called, "Hello, Yoshi."

"Newt! Hello!" Yoshi put down the axe and walked out to meet us. Face to face, they seemed awkward with each other. What would it be like to have your government tell you that your friend was now your enemy?

Newt presented me to Yoshi as his "cousin" and introduced Cat and Draggin as my friends visiting from Vancouver.

Yoshi's eyes widened. "Good names! What brings you to our house?"

"Well, we hoped to talk to your father. Maddy is interested in shadow puppets, and I told her your father is an expert. Is he here?" A rather shaky cover story, but we didn't have much to work with.

"Father's working in the shed," Yoshi replied.

I was afraid that Yoshi would ask me about where I lived, and I'd blow it by talking about something that didn't exist in 1941. I didn't have to worry, though, because Newt kept up a steady chatter with Yoshi, telling him everything he'd missed at school in the last two weeks. Although Japan's attack on Pearl Harbour had to have been the main topic of discussion, Newt didn't mention it.

As we entered the work shed, Mr. Tagawa put down the tool he was repairing and stood up. He was average height, a bit on the skinny side, and had short hair. He brushed off his pants—although they looked pretty clean to me—and smiled.

"Hello," he said. Yoshi made introductions, and Mr. Tagawa shook hands with each of us.

Newt told Mr. Tagawa about my "interest" in shadow puppets. His face brightened at the mention of a favourite topic. He invited us to lunch, then turned to put away his tools.

At the house, we were welcomed by Yoshi's mother. She had kind eyes, and I felt comfortable with her right away, even though she spoke little. Her long hair was gathered into a bun, and she wore a well-used apron over a plain blue dress. Yoshi introduced us to his two younger sisters and baby brother.

Mr. Tagawa joined us and brought out a beautiful hand-carved trunk that looked very old. He opened it and pulled out a black paper cut-out of a man. It was attached to a stick. Next, he took out a dragon, and everyone laughed and clapped Draggin on the back.

The puppets were kind of like jack-o-lanterns—parts that are cut away become visible with light from behind. Some of the human puppets were walking, and some had tiny sticks attached to movable arms. One had its hands on its hips, one appeared to be running, and another wore a robe and a tall hat. There were nonhuman forms as well; a pig, a cat, and a fish. Finally, Mr. Tagawa laid out a horse and cart, and even a house.

He explained in his slow, formal English how the puppets worked: the light shone from behind them and cast their shadows onto a screen. I'd seen shadow puppets before, but I pretended they were new to me and asked as many questions as I could think of. Mr. Tagawa answered politely. When I ran out of questions, he announced that it was time to eat and carefully repacked them into the trunk.

We settled at the table Mrs. Tagawa had set with bread, dried fish, and tea. I tried to eat slowly in spite of my ravenous hunger.

As I listened to Mr. Tagawa talk about his favourite plays, I let my eyes wander about the cabin and noted the differences between this home and present-day

Cortes homes. Even people who came to the island only for summers had far more belongings than the Tagawas. Yet, I couldn't think of anything they needed. I looked at the wooden shelf that held the family's dishes and noted that every single mug they owned had been put to use. In fact, Mr. and Mrs. Tagawa were sharing one. My mom's good set of dishes that we use only at Christmas and Thanksgiving has twelve of everything: twelve plates, twelve cups, and so on. And we've never once had twelve people eat at our house at the same time.

The Tagawas' loft was connected to the main floor by a stairway that was more of a ladder than a proper staircase. The three older children slept there. Imagine sleeping with your siblings every night. It must be comforting to never wake up alone.

Yoshi's sisters, Nami and Fumi, had finished eating and were playing quietly in the loft, peeking over the side every once in a while to giggle at the visitors. They were six and eight years old, yet seemed so much younger than Yoshi. Their baby brother, Mitsuo, stayed close to his mother, always touching her skirt or at least her chair, and watched the strangers with curious but cautious eyes.

Mrs. Tagawa spoke softly to Yoshi, who turned to us. "Mother needs water; I'm behind in my chores. Please excuse me for a moment."

"I'll help," Newt said, and the two of them left the cabin.

I continued to look around at the family's belongings, neatly arranged on the few shelves. It reminded me of a story I'd read in school about the internment. Some local kids had peeked in the windows of a house after the Japanese Canadian occupants had been forced to leave. I remembered the description of dishes still stacked carefully on the shelves because that particular family had been given only one hour's notice to pack.

I recalled how I'd felt, reading that story, and how outraged and sad I'd been, imagining my own family being forced to leave our lives behind without knowing where we were going. All those feelings returned, but the Tagawas weren't black and white photos in a textbook—they were real. *These* white plates might soon be left behind on *this* red shelf. *This* real life family would be sent away.

I looked at Mrs. Tagawa, carrying the baby as she moved quietly about the kitchen. I watched Fumi and Nami playing, and suddenly, I knew what we had to do.

"Cat," I whispered. "Get Draggin. We need to talk."

# CHAPTER 12
# THE MESSAGE

"I'm sure now!" I said as the three of us huddled around the corner of the house. "I absolutely-for-sure know that we are here to warn the Tagawas about the internment. In fact, we're here to convince them to leave. And that's why we couldn't get back before."

"How can you be so sure, Maddy?" Cat asked.

"It makes sense. We've arrived just before the internment, so there's still time for the Tagawas to get away. And our story is believable because Pearl Harbour's happened, so some of it's already started." My eagerness grew as I talked.

Cat, familiar with this scenario, tugged at my reins. "Slow down, Maddy. Don't get ahead of yourself. Have we even decided the whole message thing is real?"

Draggin spoke. "Must be, or we would have gone back yesterday, right?"

"Not necessarily," Cat said. "What if the gate is open only for those five days in August? What if the reason we couldn't go back is because we have to wait until it's August over here."

"No!" My panic pushed forward. "That's not right. It doesn't matter what the date is here. It's the full moon."

"You only want that to be true, Maddy," Cat said quietly.

I took a breath to calm myself, let it out slowly, and said, "But we agree we have to try the portal again in the next few nights—close to the full moon, right?" Cat and Draggin both nodded, so I continued. "And it is possible that we have to deliver a message in order to go back, right?" They nodded again, but more slowly. "And the only message that makes sense is to warn the Tagawas. Remember, no one else knows what's going to happen besides us."

The twins looked at each other and did their talking-without-talking thing. "So, what do we do now?" Cat asked.

"We tell Newt," I answered and started walking toward the well.

While Yoshi finished his chores, we told Newt about our mission. But, of course, that meant we had to educate him about the internment.

Once again Draggin began the story. With the faces of the Tagawa family in my mind, it seemed more real now, and every word made me angry.

"After the New Year, they will begin to take the men to work camps." Draggin's voice slowed. "A few were taken in December, in fact." He swallowed. "I guess they're already gone."

Newt struggled to take it in. "Why would anyone suspect the Tagawas? How could one family, on an island way up here, be a threat to the safety of Canada?"

No one answered.

"How will you help them?" Newt asked. This started a discussion that went back and forth for several minutes.

In the end we decided the Tagawas' best hope would be to get their boat unlocked and leave. As soon as possible.

Newt sat quietly for a while, and then the cloud of sadness and confusion seemed to lift somewhat. "We have to tell Yoshi everything. We won't be able to convince Mr. and Mrs. Tagawa without him."

"Everything?" I asked doubtfully.

"Everything," he said firmly.

Once we'd gathered in the shed, Newt began. "You know that old Indian legend the teacher told us about the lagoon messenger?" he asked Yoshi.

"Yes," Yoshi said.

"Well, these three are messengers. Maddy's not really my cousin. They're visiting alright, but from the future!"

Yoshi's eyebrows went up slightly, and then he nodded.

"Did you hear what I said? These three are from the twenty-first century!" Newt was waving his arms wildly.

"Yes, I figured it was something . . . extraordinary," Yoshi said.

"You're kidding! How did you know?" I asked.

"Your clothes—obviously borrowed—your strange shoes, Draggin's wristwatch, the way you talk. And a strong . . . feeling."

"I know what you mean," I said with a shiver.

"So," Yoshi said tentatively. "What message have you brought?"

Cat sat down beside Yoshi. "You really believe us? Just like that? It's kinda weird how well you're taking this."

Yoshi and Newt exchanged looks. Newt spoke first. "Some people believe in magic and some don't. Yoshi and I both do," he said firmly. "It's one of the reasons we're friends, right, Yoshi?"

"Yes," said Yoshi. "I don't doubt that you are messengers. However, I suspect your message is not a happy one."

Cat touched his arm. "Bad times are coming for Japanese Canadians, Yoshi. Very bad times."

Yoshi swallowed and nodded. "I hear my parents talking late at night about what the attack on Pearl Harbour will mean for us. They're worried." He looked down at the floor. "What's going to happen to us?" he asked quietly.

Draggin pulled his stool close to Yoshi's. "All Japanese Canadians who live within a hundred miles of the west coast will be forced to move. Men will be taken first. To work in camps and to build roads. Then whole families will be moved next spring—to old abandoned mining towns or camps." He paused to let Yoshi absorb this.

"Where will my family go?" he asked.

"We don't know. People are sent all over the country."

"What about our farm and our boat?" Yoshi's voice wavered.

"The government workers will promise to protect your things, but . . ." Draggin could hardly bring himself to say it. I thought of the Tagawas' freshly painted boat. Then I thought of the picture in my textbook of hundreds of fishing boats tied carelessly together, many left to sink.

"But it's a lie," Draggin continued. "You have to get away from here, Yoshi, as soon as possible. Maybe your father can sell his land to a friend and get them to take care of it for you. I don't know. But they are going to come for your father, and then you might not see him again for years. And the rest of you will be sent to a camp. We have to convince your parents to get away from the coast."

Yoshi sat still, head down, hands folded in his lap. When he raised his face, tear tracks stained his cheeks, but his eyes snapped angrily. "What if we refuse to go?"

I bit my lip. I'd always thought it would be so cool to see history for myself, but I hadn't felt this awful since the day Grandpa died. I blinked back tears as Cat put her hand on Yoshi's arm again and said, "The community leaders will decide that it shows loyalty to cooperate. You can't win, Yoshi. I know this seems like the time to fight, but for us, this is done; sad facts in our history books. We can't change the big picture, but we can change the outcome for your family."

Yoshi dropped his head again and let his tears come. The air was heavy with sadness. Finally, he sat up straight, wiped his face on his sleeve, and said, "Okay. We must convince Father that we need to leave. You have to tell him everything you've told me, and I'll interpret to be sure he understands."

"Do you think he'll believe us?" Cat asked Yoshi. "I mean, we really need to be convincing if he's going to leave behind his home and take his family into hiding. How are we gonna do that?"

"How about my watch?" asked Draggin. "If we show him something that's obviously from the future . . ."

"Just because he's never seen one doesn't mean it's from the future. There's a big world out there," Cat said.

We sat and thought. Yoshi spoke first. "We need to make father feel the magic he believes in—deep in his heart." His mouth twisted as he chewed the inside of his cheek. Then his face brightened slightly. "I know! The shadow puppets. He believes they're magical and sometimes deliver important messages. The puppets will cast the spell we need."

Yoshi went to the house and returned with the trunk. He laid it carefully on the workbench. Away from Mr. Tagawa's watchful eyes, we felt more comfortable taking a closer look.

Cat ran her fingers across the pattern on the lid of the trunk. "This looks Chinese," she murmured.

"It is," said Yoshi. "My great grandfather brought it home from China when he was in the army."

Yoshi turned to face us. His fear and anger had been replaced by determination.

"You know, when I grow up I am going to be a motion picture director. I will live in Hollywood and work with great actors like Humphrey Bogart." Newt smiled and nodded, and the rest of us looked at each other and shrugged. Yoshi continued, "Here is what we have to do . . ."

And he started to outline the most important show of his life.

# CHAPTER 13
# REHEARSAL

"What's the play about, Yoshi?" asked Nami. She and Fumi watched Yoshi as he carefully unpacked the trunk. Their hands were clasped behind their backs obediently; their feet danced with excitement. When Fumi reached out to touch a puppet, Yoshi clucked his tongue at her, and the little hand whipped back as her dancing feet sped up.

He outlined the story for the girls. They looked at each other and giggled happily. "What should we do, Yoshi?"

"First, Fumi can lend me her blanket," he said. Fumi hesitated, pulling her tattered baby blanket close to her chest. Then she thrust it toward her big brother.

"Thank you." He set it carefully on the work bench. "You will both be puppeteers, like father when he puts on a show for us. Can you do that?"

They both nodded happily.

"You must be gentle—don't touch the cut-outs, only the sticks." He handed each girl a puppet, and they stopped dancing and fidgeting and stood as if frozen, staring in awe at the angular figures. Yoshi continued to pull forms gently out of the trunk and lay them on the workbench. We were all anxious to see them "on stage."

Yoshi handed me a white sheet and asked me to hang it in front of the workbench. Cat and I worked together to string a line. Everything seemed to be taking too long. "Do you really think this is necessary?" I asked no one in particular. "Do we have time for this?"

Yoshi stopped what he was doing. "We're asking my parents to leave behind their life's work. The play will help my father's heart to remember the magic. Trust me—it's the only way."

By the time we finished hanging the sheet, Newt and Draggin had boarded up the windows, and Yoshi had taken everything out of the trunk.

"What do we do for light behind the screen?" I asked, thinking about the ease of flipping on a projector.

"We place lanterns behind the sheet. The puppets go between the light and the sheet—almost touching is best, but further back for bigger images. You'll see."

I sat down on the floor in front of the workbench while Yoshi placed three lanterns behind me. He handed me a puppet, which I held above my head, close to the sheet. "How does it look?" I asked.

Newt and Draggin went to stand with Cat and the little girls. Yoshi turned up the lanterns, and everyone gasped as each detail of the cut-out came to life on the sheet.

Yoshi and I switched places. Yoshi moved the puppets the way he had watched his father do so many times, and suddenly two people walked side by side across the screen.

"Excellent!" I exclaimed. "Now all we need is a script."

Yoshi's voice drifted out from behind the puppet stage. "Once when the world was old and wise, but humans were new, there was a beautiful lagoon where the people came to dig for clams and pick the berries along the shore."

Suddenly a pool of water appeared on the sheet.

"Hey, how did you do that?" I poked my head "backstage" to see Fumi's blanket bunched up on a high stool, casting a perfect lagoon-shaped shadow.

Everyone got involved then, trying different items behind the sheet to see how things looked. Yoshi repeated the first part of the story quickly, and then we worked together to add the second half.

When we were happy with the script, Yoshi unwrapped a small shamisen from a quilt. It looked something like a guitar—a small rectangular body attached to an extra-long neck. From the trunk, Yoshi pulled a triangular piece of wood he called a bachi and began to pick the strings with it. At first I thought it sounded like a banjo, but as Yoshi got warmed up, the notes he plucked began to soften and melt together. I closed my eyes and listened to the sad, gentle voice of the shamisen. After a few moments, Yoshi began to talk softly in Japanese as he played, and his story floated on the notes like a leaf on the breeze.

The girls listened to Yoshi and prompted me as the Japanese words wafted through the shed. When I got lost, Nami would give me a new puppet or gently move my hand in the right direction, and I would find my place again.

When Yoshi stopped, no one moved for a moment, and the magic faded away with the final notes of the shamisen.

"We're ready," Yoshi said.

# CHAPTER 14

# SONG OF THE SHAMISEN

By the time Mr. and Mrs. Tagawa and Mitsuo seated themselves in the shed, the grey sky had darkened deeply. We closed the door, shutting out the last of the light, and turned up the lanterns. The little girls and I sat cross-legged on the floor between the curtain and the work-bench, and Cat and Draggin were at either end of the sheet to hand us puppets and props. Yoshi sat down on a stool to play the shamisen.

Every note trembled softly, and it seemed that the music itself lulled us away to a world where anything was possible—even visitors from another time. Yoshi began to talk over the music, and his voice had a soft rhythm that had not been there during rehearsal. I had to concentrate to make sure I didn't miss my first cue, as the puppets made their way to the lagoon. Although I didn't understand his words, Yoshi's story stretched itself out on the music like a cat on a warm stove. My hands became the puppets, bringing his words to life with a magic of their own.

*Once when the world was old and wise, but humans were new, there was a beautiful lagoon where the people came to dig clams and pick berries along the shore. On a warm summer day, with children playing near the mouth of the lagoon where the water hurried through in a cool rush, mothers, grandmothers, and older children carefully plucked juicy blackberries from the jealous bushes. Suddenly, a cry of surprise rang out, and everyone turned toward the water. Right where the lagoon's mouth widened into a laugh, a head bobbed along on the current and floated into the heart of the lagoon. Already, several of the mothers were wading into the water. Which child had fallen in? But then, a figure emerged from the water, and before them stood a stranger. Although he didn't speak, they knew right away he had come from the Creator.*

*He stayed only two days but showed them secret places to find food so the people would never be hungry. When the time came for him to go, he swam to the great rock in the mouth of the lagoon and dove into the fast water. He disappeared without a trace, back to the Creator.*

*For many years, the people returned to the lagoon at the same time and waited patiently for the messenger to return, but he did not. Over time, fewer and fewer people went to wait, and although the story of the messenger remained a favourite around the fire, it became a tradition of remembering rather than waiting.*

*Many lifetimes later, a wise woman came to the lagoon on a warm summer's eve at the ripe moon and the high tide. She sat alone under a great fir tree, and as the tide reached its peak, three heads appeared out of nowhere and floated into the lagoon. Before the woman stood three messengers who told her that they had a message for one special family.*

*The messengers visited the family by the lake to tell them that danger lay ahead. Already, trouble had visited; the family boat sat locked to the dock. In the city, the government had shut down the newspapers and schools of the people, and worst of all, the rumoured evacuation was coming, the messengers said.*

*The family accepted this news sadly and made preparations to leave their beloved home. They climbed into their boat and sailed away to safety, just before a great storm of sadness and despair struck the coast with a force that would be felt for a hundred years.*

*This is the story of the lagoon messengers and how they saved the Tagawas.*

As the final notes of the shamisen floated on the air, Mitsuo climbed down off his mother's lap. Giggling and clapping, he tottered around the sheet to uncover the magic. Nami and Fumi, still unaware of anything other than a make-believe show for their parents, showed the puppets to Mitsuo and tried to keep his eager little fingers away from the delicate cut-outs.

Mr. and Mrs. Tagawa hadn't moved as we stepped from behind the sheet to face them. Mr. Tagawa studied us with such intensity that I blushed. Mrs. Tagawa sat perfectly still except for her hands fluttering over each other in her lap. Her eyes were fixed on Yoshi. Finally, Mr. Tagawa spoke.

"Excuse us, please." He turned to Yoshi and a stream of words erupted from him. The conversation whipped back and forth in Japanese, with Mrs. Tagawa joining in occasionally.

Finally, Yoshi turned to us. "My father believes you are messengers but begs for some evidence of these future events you warn of. He says he cannot uproot his family and chance losing his farm without some proof of your story."

We looked at each other. What proof could we offer?

Draggin stepped forward with his left arm extended. He took off his watch and demonstrated a few features while Mr. and Mrs. Tagawa asked questions.

Eventually Mr. and Mrs. Tagawa and the three children headed for the door of the work shed. The last to leave, Mr. Tagawa turned back.

"Your mother and I will talk more about your story," he said to Yoshi, who nodded and rubbed his hands together anxiously.

We cleaned up in silence. Yoshi put the puppets back in the trunk while Cat and I took down and refolded the white sheet.

As Newt unboarded the windows, Draggin said, "Hey, what's that?" He stared out into the darkness with his nose squashed against the cold glass of the window.

I joined him. "I can't see a thing," I said. "What is it?"

"A light," he said. "Definitely. Way down there past the house. Isn't that the direction we came from?"

Yoshi stood beside us now—his face close to the glass. "Yes," he said. "There's definitely a light. Someone's walking toward the house." His voice grew tighter with each word.

My mind flashed to Crazy Bill and his shotgun. "Draggin, can you tell who it is? Are they carrying anything?"

"Um, they're not very tall and . . . yes, they're carrying something besides the lantern!" Draggin turned toward us, his face pale. "Could be Crazy Bill," he said.

We'd told Yoshi a bit about last night's misadventure—enough for him to understand that we were all in danger if Crazy Bill had followed us.

"What do we do?" My heart pounded. "We can't charge out there and startle him, or he might start shooting. But we have to warn your parents, or they'll let him in!" The light bobbed closer and closer to the house.

"Come on, let's go but be quiet!" I opened the shed door, and we made our way across the grass as silently as we could. On the other side of the house, the lantern approached quickly.

When we got close, I stopped and peered into the gloom. Cat ran into the back of me, and I stumbled forward. The lantern stopped, and we all froze. I held my breath and hoped for a miracle.

# CHAPTER 15

# BOAT DAY NEWS

"There you are. Hello." Malila waved the lantern at us, and we all stood panting with relief for a second before rushing forward to greet her.

"What are you doing here?" I asked.

"The baby came quickly. Good birth." What Draggin had mistaken for a gun barrel turned out to be a rolled up newspaper, which she waved at us. "Today was boat day. Plenty of news from the city. Crazy Bill showed up, too, with some news of his own." She held her lantern close to each of us and did a quick inspection. "You okay?" she asked.

"Yes, we're fine," I said. "Newt saved us from Crazy Bill, and we finally got here this morning. I'll tell you about it later." I couldn't stop grinning at her. "What news do you have?"

Malila grunted and waved her hand at me. "I need to talk to Mrs. and Mr. Tagawa," she said. "And I need to sit down."

We went into the house, and Mr. and Mrs. Tagawa stood to greet yet another unexpected guest. Yoshi brought her a stool, and I gave Malila a quick summary of the play we had just performed for the Tagawas.

"You were right about the message!" I whispered in her ear.

Malila turned to the Tagawas. She told them how she'd seen us appear out of nowhere at the lagoon. Mr. Tagawa nodded solemnly, then asked if Malila believed the rest of the story—the part about the Japanese families being moved.

"We watched the police lock up your boat yesterday," she said. She handed the newspaper to Yoshi. "Steamship came today. There was lots of talk when people read this."

Yoshi opened the *Vancouver Daily Province*. He read silently while the rest of us waited. Then he looked at his parents with such sorrow, and when he spoke quietly in Japanese, it sounded as though most of the air had been squeezed from his lungs. Mrs. and Mr. Tagawa sat motionless as they listened to their son.

Yoshi handed the paper to me, and I laid it on the kitchen table so the rest of us could read it. The facts were familiar, and I may have read a copy of this exact article in my textbook, but my stomach fell with every announcement: 1200 boats had been impounded; all Japanese language schools had been closed; and Japanese newspapers were being shut down. The article also mentioned rumours of a complete "evacuation" of all Japanese Canadians from the west coast. For their own safety, the article said. In case white people retaliated against any spies.

My eyes burned. How infuriating to be here and *still* feel so helpless. I already knew that not one single spy would ever be found.

The Tagawas would not go to a prison camp. Not if I could help it.

Mr. Tagawa cleared his throat. "We will plan to go."

Relief washed over me for a second, and then Malila spoke again.

"We'll find a way to keep your farm safe. But there's more bad news; Crazy Bill also visited the dock, telling everyone he caught some spies yesterday, but they got away." She looked at me with raised eyebrows. "I think it's not safe for any of you. Everyone should go. Soon."

I called a conference with the twins, and we stepped outside and huddled together on the porch. "What time is it now?" I asked Draggin.

"Almost six o'clock," he said. "We can still make it back for high tide."

Cat nodded. "Yes, I think we should get back to the lagoon and go home. I've been thinking about our parents and how we're, you know, missing! Can you imagine how freaked they must be? We have to try tonight."

The door opened, and Yoshi stepped out. "My father says we will go tomorrow." Grief tugged at his eyes and mouth. "Mother asks that you stay tonight as our guests."

I looked at Cat and Draggin, unsure what to say.

The door opened again, and Malila joined us on the crowded porch.

"What are you doing out here?" she asked.

"Trying to figure out what to do!" My anxiety had spiked again after Cat mentioned our own world and what might be happening there. Our folks probably thought we'd been kidnapped.

"Well, nothing to do until tomorrow. Might as well sleep." Malila nodded as if to end the discussion.

"No!" said Cat. "We have to get home. We need to get back to the lagoon tonight, Malila. Can you help us?"

Malila reached out and stroked Cat's face gently. "We should stay here tonight. It is too far for me to go back when I just got here, and you can't go on your own. Tomorrow, we help with the packing. Then we go to the boat."

She smiled and patted the top of Cat's head—something Cat would never tolerate from anyone else.

"We still have a couple more nights to try to get back through the gate, right?" asked Cat.

Draggin counted on his fingers. "We came two nights before full moon, spent the first night at Malila's, next one at Crazy Bill's, and tonight it's full. So, if our 'several days' theory is correct, we should have a couple more nights to get back before the portal closes." He looked at us. "Assuming we don't have to wait until next August."

"Shut up!" Cat and I cried together, and Cat punched him. Then she turned to Malila.

"You're right, Malila. Maybe it's not such a good idea to try to get back tonight." Cat shuddered. She was probably thinking of Crazy Bill.

"Good," said Malila. "I'll go tell them we're staying to help." She and Yoshi went back inside. Out in the garden, the winter kale and the thyme seemed to shiver with me.

"First we make sure they get away safely. Then we'll worry about ourselves." It felt right, even as I said it, and I could tell from their faces that Cat and Draggin agreed.

We opened the door and returned to the warmth of the fire. But my mind raced with images of my mom and grandma, sick with worry.

Mrs. Tagawa asked me to take the three little ones to play in the loft while she made dinner, and I asked Draggin to help me entertain them.

"Would you like a story?" Draggin asked them. Still excited from the puppet play, the children were eager for another tale. They sat with me on the blankets while Draggin told them his all-time favourite story: Why the Dragon is part of the Chinese zodiac and the Cat is not.

"Once upon a time, the gods announced the creation of the zodiac. They invited the animals who might like to be part of it to come to the temple the next morning at dawn where twelve animals would be chosen to be symbols on the zodiac. Well, Cat and Mouse, who were great friends back then, decided to go together. 'Wake me up in time, Mouse, and we will go to the temple. Surely we will both be chosen for the zodiac.' Mouse agreed, and they both went to bed.

"In the morning Cat awoke, stretched lazily, and then remembered the big event. The sun sat high in the sky. She had overslept! Mouse had not come to wake Cat, and she missed the meeting. And so, while there is a year of the mouse on the zodiac, there is no year of the cat. And, of course, Mouse and Cat have been enemies ever since. Oh, and naturally, the mighty Dragon was chosen by the gods, and the best people are born in the year of the Dragon! The end."

The children giggled and clapped, and Draggin grinned at me. I'd heard it before, of course. But when he told it with Cat around, he really emphasized the part about the cat being outsmarted by the mouse.

Much to my surprise, Draggin knew lots of children's games, and the sound of laughter thinned the gloominess that hung over everyone else.

At dinner, we sat on the floor in a circle around the stove since there weren't enough chairs. Mrs. Tagawa served the kids first, with big bowls of steaming hot soup, and then poured smaller portions into mugs for the adults. After the experiences of the last few days, I would never take another meal for granted; I ate the soup gratefully and wondered how much stretching Mrs. Tagawa had done to make it go around. She also made rice balls to go with the soup, and we polished off every last one. Cat, Draggin, and I ate the most. Mr. and Mrs. Tagawa and Yoshi ate little and spoke less.

After dinner, Mr. Tagawa and Yoshi went to the shed to begin organizing things there. In the house, Cat and Newt did the dishes with Malila while Draggin and I took the children back up to the loft to play. Mrs. Tagawa continued her own sorting, checking to make sure the children weren't paying too much attention to what she was doing.

Our eyes met and she smiled sadly. She pointed to her three children, who played happily, oblivious to the turn their lives were about to take. "We will tell them tomorrow," she said to me, and I nodded.

I turned back to Draggin and joined in the game. Keeping them distracted suddenly seemed like an important job.

Within the hour, Mrs. Tagawa called to the children and spoke quietly to them in Japanese. The girls groaned in the universal language of kids at bedtime. Mitsuo, who had already begun rubbing his eyes, climbed down into the arms of his mother, who hugged him extra tight and took him into the bedroom. Nami and Fumi climbed down as well and went to wash up.

It took some planning to provide a bed for everyone, but Malila and Mrs. Tagawa managed to find a soft spot for each of us. Up in the loft, Mrs. Tagawa tucked in the girls, who snuggled close together and drifted off on their mother's lullaby. I sat with the others by the stove and imagined what she might be thinking as she watched her children sleep. Her eyes glistened when she finally climbed back down the ladder, but she resumed her sorting without a word.

Exhausted, Yoshi and his father returned from the shed. We made room for them by the fire, and everyone sat silently for a while.

Then Mr. Tagawa spoke. "Tell us about the future. Your present."

I looked at the others. Who felt like storytelling in the midst of this sadness? Cat saved us again.

"Well," she began. "In our time, everyone has electricity. And we have computers which answer our questions about anything in a few seconds." She stopped when she saw the look on Mr. Tagawa's face. He turned to Yoshi and spoke in Japanese.

Yoshi asked Cat how everyone could "have" a computer. Didn't the computers live in their own homes? Were they slaves or something?

The three of us burst out laughing, and Cat began again, being more precise in her explanation. Many questions followed the revelation of a book-sized machine that could do everything Cat described.

Cat said she felt more connected to her own family history here in the past. "My grandfather tells us stories of his childhood in Chinatown. He was born in 1947. Hey, if we went to Vancouver, we could meet our great-grandparents!" She and Draggin grinned at each other. "Where did you grow up, Mr. Tagawa?" she asked.

Mr. Tagawa had also grown up in Vancouver. His voice resonated with fondness as he talked of Powell Street, also known as *Little Tokyo*. He spoke of his first job as a delivery boy for the Nakamura florist shop in 1922 when he was a few years older than Yoshi. He described waiting for his father outside the Imperial Hotel and eating red candied ginger with his friends.

He had such a happy-sad expression on his face and looked at the ceiling as though he could see Powell Street laid out before him. I could almost see it myself.

Mr. Tagawa suggested we go to sleep so we could get an early start in the morning. No one argued. I was exhausted after the events and emotions of the day, not to mention our nearly sleepless night in the woodshed.

Malila, Cat, and I got comfortable on the bed of blankets arranged on the floor in front of the fire, and Newt and Draggin went up to the loft with Yoshi. Mr. and Mrs. Tagawa disappeared into the bedroom, and the cabin fell quiet.

I wiggled closer to Cat so I wouldn't disturb the others and asked if she was still awake.

"Barely," she whispered.

"I'm sorry I ever argued with you about everybody's Different being the same. Really sorry. I get it now."

"We'll see," she said softly.

"What do you mean?" I asked.

"Well, if you actually make an effort to get along with your stepdad, I'll know you get it."

In spite of my confusion, I felt annoyed. "What are you talking about? What does Grunt have to do with any of this?"

"Everything, Maddy. You won't even try to get along with him because you're uncomfortable with his Different. That's how it starts. You put enough of those things together and then when scary stuff happens—like a war—it turns into fear and then into hatred, and before you know it, you've got nice people like the Tagawas in prison camps."

"Not the same thing, Cat," I muttered through clenched teeth and turned my back to her. It took me a long time to fall asleep, partly because I had to cool off, but mostly because I felt kinda sick. I was thinking about whether we'd get back. About the Tagawas. About the other families this would tear apart. About this whole big, crazy, horrible internment and all the discrimination still in the world.

And about Grant.

# CHAPTER 16

# THE MOB

The morning held a series of tiny heartbreaks: Fumi and Nami each picking one toy to take, tears streaming down their confused faces; Mrs. Tagawa moving through the cabin, touching every surface, rubbing the curtains between her fingers and smelling the fabric, committing her home to the memory of her senses; and Yoshi carefully repacking the puppets into the trunk, shoulders shaking softly, trying to hide his tears. I did what I could: I entertained the girls and Mitsuo, I packed boxes, and I cleaned. And when it came time, I helped load the wagon, which Mr. Tagawa and Yoshi brought to the front of the house, already half-filled with tools and crates from the shed.

With the wagon as full as possible, Mr. Tagawa and Yoshi climbed up onto the seat. They would load the boat, then return for the family. Mrs. Tagawa took the three little ones back into the cabin as Yoshi looked down at Newt and the twins and me. "We'll need help, but there's room for only two, father says."

The twins' hands had a quick conversation, and Cat said, "We'll stay and help Mrs. Tagawa if you like."

Yoshi nodded. Newt and I climbed onto the back of the wagon, and Mr. Tagawa spoke to the big Clydesdale. The wagon jerked with the horse's first step, and I nearly toppled off the crate I was sitting on. I shifted over and hung on to the sideboard.

Newt and I, bouncing along uncomfortably in the back of the wagon, discussed the Tagawas over the clatter of the wheels and the rattling of the boxes, barrels, and crates. Where would they go? How would they get what they needed? Would their property be safe? Would they ever come back? I remembered from school that very few of the interned families ever returned to the coast.

At the dock, Mr. Tagawa spoke only to give orders to Yoshi. He climbed into the hold to pack the supplies as efficiently as possible, as they would need every square inch. A boat meant for fishing trips might be comfortable for two people below. It would be horribly crowded for the six of them.

Newt and I carried the boxes from the wagon to the boat and handed them on board to Yoshi, who passed them down to his father in the hold. Several of the crates we had to carry together, struggling down the ramp to the lower dock.

We pushed one especially heavy crate onto the boat, then stopped to catch our breath. I looked around for the first time and saw a man watching us from the boat across the dock.

"Hi, Mr. James," Newt said. The man nodded, saying nothing. I looked around and saw others watching along the dock. Newt said hello to those he knew and got only nods in return. I wished we hadn't noticed the watchers. I felt uncomfortable and picked up the pace in spite of my tired legs. The sooner we finished, the better.

When Mr. Tagawa finally emerged from the hold, he told Yoshi to wait in the wagon while he climbed down another ladder into the engine room.

As the three of us returned to the wagon, Newt announced he had to get home. He'd have some explaining to do, he told us. His parents hadn't been too happy about Newt visiting the Tagawas overnight in the first place, but he'd promised to be home by noon, which was several hours ago.

He shook Yoshi's hand. "Good luck, Yoshi." He looked as though he wanted to say something else but couldn't quite find the words. He smiled at his friend as best he could. Then he turned to me. "Good luck to you, too," he said and walked off the dock.

I watched him go, knowing I'd never forget the boy I knew for only a day.

I rubbed my arms, which tingled from carrying heavy boxes. I was going to be sore tomorrow.

Tomorrow. What would tomorrow look like? Where would we be? *When* would we be?

Mr. Tagawa emerged from the engine room, checked a few things on deck, and hopped off the boat. He strode past the watchers as though he hadn't noticed them and climbed the ramp to the wagon on the upper dock.

By the time we got back to the house, the sun had set. Cat and Draggin played with Nami and Fumi on the front porch as the wagon pulled up. Yoshi told his father that he would tend to the horse, but Mr. Tagawa shook his head and walked away slowly, talking to the big animal as he stroked its sweaty side.

I told the twins about loading the boat. And about the watchers. "How did it go here?" I asked.

"It's been pretty sad." Cat looked at Yoshi. "Your mom's been really quiet. She hardly looked at us the whole time we finished packing. And the girls don't really seem to understand what's going on. They're upset one minute and excited about the trip the next."

We went into the house and found Mrs. Tagawa sitting in the rocking chair with Mitsuo on her lap. She sang softly to him in Japanese but stopped when we came in.

My breath caught. The house was so empty. In the shadows of the far corner, trunks and crates sat like large, patient animals. Most of the family's possessions would be left behind, packed away in this dark alcove.

Mr. Tagawa stood in the doorway. The room grew quiet as he took a last look at the home he'd built for his family. There were lines in his forehead and around his mouth that I hadn't noticed before.

He spoke quickly, then turned abruptly and left.

Yoshi translated: "We're to load this stuff into the wagon. Then we'll go to Malila's house for supper and then . . ." He turned to his sisters. "Say goodbye to the house now," he said softly. He grabbed the closest box and strode out the door.

The twins and I carried the last items out of the house to the wagon and handed them up to Mr. Tagawa. Finally, with everyone settled, Mr. Tagawa grabbed the reins. He did not look back, but I did, silently watching the house grow smaller and smaller until a curve in the trail swept it from my view.

At Malila's, we climbed slowly out of the wagon. Malila had the fire roaring and she and Mrs. Tagawa cooked together silently. During the meal of stew and bannock, the only sound was spoon against bowl.

Malila made a small bed of blankets by the fire, not unlike the one she'd made for Cat and Draggin and me the night we arrived. Fumi, Nami, and Mitsuo lay down to sleep in their clothes. The rest of us sat quietly, listening to the crackling fire.

At about eleven o'clock, the parents roused the children and helped them out to the wagon where they sat sleepily, cuddled around their mother. Malila came with us for the short ride from her house to the dock.

I looked out at the filling lagoon. It wouldn't be long now. For the first time all day, I let my thoughts return to our own situation. We would be leaving soon after the Tagawas, and this world, which had become so real and so important to me, would be gone in the blink of an eye. Or at least I hoped so. What a strange sensation to desperately want something that would cause me grief.

When we got to the dock, we lit the candles inside our bug lights—tin cans with holes cut into the sides. The moon helped, but clouds scudded across it, causing the light to pulse unevenly like a bulb with a bad connection.

We moved as quietly as possible, carrying the last few boxes containing the family's past, present, and future. Below, Mrs. Tagawa got the three younger children settled into one bunk, which left an impossibly tiny corner for Yoshi. We'd almost emptied the wagon when Malila whispered at me from her position as lookout: "Somebody's coming."

I looked past her to the road. Small points of light bobbed down the hill toward the dock. My heart jumped into my throat.

The watchers!

I leapt out of the wagon and ran to Mr. Tagawa, who crouched on the dock, cutting the chain off the boat with a hacksaw. I nudged him carefully and pointed at the small parade of lights bouncing toward us. He returned to his task without a word—his arm pulling back and forth with new urgency.

Malila called softly to the twins and me. "Go hide in the bushes at the end of the dock."

The three of us raced to the end of the dock and dove into the bushes just before the mob arrived. Cat and I were on one side, and Draggin was on the other. I held my breath as the lights came closer and closer.

The sound of the hacksaw stopped, and the chain clattered onto the dock. As the crowd passed by us, I could just make out about a dozen people, most carrying sacks. One of the smaller shapes looked familiar, and then I heard the unmistakeable sound of Newt's voice. "We better hurry, Pop. He's starting the engine."

I heard it too—the engine sputtered but didn't catch. What was happening? I was preparing to jump out of my hiding spot when I felt Cat's hand on my arm. She whispered in my ear, "Let's wait and see what happens."

The boat engine caught and, over the chugging, came Newt's voice amplified by the water. "Yoshi, wait. Stop!"

My heart pounded in my ears. I couldn't stand it. I started to get up, then stopped as the boat engine suddenly died.

"Try it again," Yoshi's frightened voice floated to us. Mr. Tagawa, his voice tight, snapped back at Yoshi in Japanese and tried the engine again. It wouldn't turn over.

"That's it!" I cried, jumping up. Cat grabbed me and pulled me back down, pointing up the road.

More lights headed toward us. Fewer this time, but moving much faster.

At the dock Newt had obviously reached the boat. "Yoshi, tell your father not to start the engine."

Yoshi's voice trembled slightly. I imagined Mr. Tagawa stepping off the boat and positioning himself between Yoshi and the crowd. I wiped my palms on my pant legs and strained to hear, while still keeping an eye on the second set of lights.

"We came to say goodbye, Yoshi. Don't look so scared!" Newt's voice carried across the water, and I let out a breath I didn't know I'd been holding.

A new voice spoke, presumably Newt's father. "Newt tells me you need to move your family. We came to tell you that we know you aren't spies like it says in the newspaper. But, if you have to go, you have to go. Christmas tomorrow. Got some extra sugar here, a few oranges—thought you could use a bit."

We heard the rustling of a sack exchanging hands, then Yoshi's, "Thank you." That sound was repeated, as one after another, people shuffled forward and handed bags of food to Yoshi, who placed each item down on the deck of the boat. Then it grew quiet.

"Well, good luck, Mr. Tagawa." It sounded like Newt's father again.

Then came Mr. Tagawa's voice, quiet but strong. "I believe that leaving is what I must do for my family. Thank you for your generous gifts. I hope to see you again soon."

The second clump of lights approached but stopped at the end of the dock, close to where we hid. Most of these men carried sacks as well, and I relaxed a little. They whispered urgently, standing in a tight group with their backs to us, rearranging the bags. One was so heavy that two men carried it between them. When they started to move again, Draggin popped out of the bushes behind them and signed frantically at us. He was practically jumping off his feet.

"What's he saying?" I asked.

Cat squinted into the dimness. "I can hardly see . . . oh crap! Crazy Bill."

## CHAPTER 17
# CRAZY BILL AGAIN

When I heard "Crazy Bill," I started moving instantly.

"Hey," I shouted as soon as my feet hit the dock. The men turned, peering into the darkness outside the lanterns' small circle of light.

"Hey, Bill. It's me and the spies. Come and get us!" Then I turned to the water and yelled as loud as I could, "Yoshi, go now!"

Mr. Tagawa tried to start the boat again. Crazy Bill and his cronies hesitated for a second, unsure which way to go, then turned and rushed down the dock.

The twins and I followed right behind them, shouting and trying to pull their attention away from the boat. The sound of the struggling engine mixed with cursing and yelling, and as the three of us arrived on the lower dock, it was chaos.

Yoshi and Newt were untying the mooring ropes while a large man, who looked a lot like Newt, squared himself up between the boat and the new arrivals. Crazy Bill yelled that Tagawa was a spy, and they'd keep him here until the police came. The heavy sack tipped out and chain rattled onto the deck. Crazy Bill grabbed the mooring ring and started to chain the boat to the dock again. Newt's dad pulled the chain out of his hands. Another man got involved, and the scene exploded into a giant scuffle of people shoving and grabbing each other.

The sound of the engine struggling and Mitsuo crying below deck added a frenzied soundtrack to the confused scene. I saw Crazy Bill push Newt's father aside and jump onto the boat. I was preparing to jump aboard, too, when someone grabbed me from behind. I tried to wrench myself free until Malila's voice spoke quietly into my ear. "Time to go."

I allowed myself to be pulled backward and managed to grab hold of Draggin as I passed him. Cat saw us and pushed through the crowd.

"We can't go now, Malila. They need us!" I cried.

"They have help," Malila said. She pointed to the dock pilings; the water approached the high tide mark. "You go now or you don't go. Hurry."

I looked back at the bizarre scene, then hugged Malila quickly.

And then it hit me. "How will we know what happens?" I asked.

"A note." Draggin grabbed Malila's hand and shouted at her. "Write a note and tell us what happens. Put it in a jar and bury it. Deep." He looked around. "Under the tree where we first met you. Okay?"

Malila nodded, then shooed us away. "Go now. Good luck, Travellers."

The three of us raced off the dock and onto the path to the spit. We ran out to the point, pulled off our outer clothing, and waded straight out into the freezing water.

"Ahh!! There's a good reason we don't swim in December!" My teeth chattered fiercely. "Cat, you go first."

"I can't!" She could barely get the words out. But Cat would follow me, and it was too cold for hesitation. I dove in and swam hard to the big rock in the middle of the lagoon's mouth.

Once I climbed up on the rock, Draggin started. He struggled against the current. The icy water had to be numbing his already exhausted arms.

He wasn't going to make it.

Just as I got to the edge of the rock, Cat dove in after him, pulling hard to catch him before he got swept away. Draggin caught her wrist in his right hand, and she started drifting.

"Not her wrist," I yelled.

Draggin could hear nothing but the unfriendly roar of the fast water. Cat tore his hand off her wrist and wrapped his arm around her waist. With both arms free now, Cat kicked hard and pulled him toward the rock. I scrambled to the lowest ledge and threw myself down on my belly. Reaching out as far as possible, I scraped my arm across a cluster of barnacles and barely felt the cuts. My fingers touched Cat's, but I couldn't grab them, and in a single beat of my heart, the twins swept past me and out into the lagoon.

# CHAPTER 18

# THE LETTER

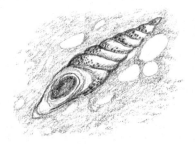

I jumped back to my feet and called Cat's name into the darkness. When I heard nothing, my mind whirled sickeningly. We had never figured out if the whole mouth of the lagoon was the doorway between times or if you had to hit the slipstream beneath the surface. Had Cat and Draggin tumbled through to our own time, or did they need to come back and dive deeper? I had no way of knowing.

I examined the water. In my frantic state, I imagined that it was beginning to slow, that it was nearly slack-tide, and soon it would be too late. I called their names over and over again and still heard nothing. The sound of the sputtering boat engine and angry voices from the dock filled my ears.

I had no more time; I had to assume they'd gotten through. I took a deep breath and raced to the top of the rock. *They made it,* I told myself firmly. *They'll be waiting for me on the other side.*

I didn't hesitate at the top; I knew where to dive, and when my feet hit the familiar hollow in the rock, I threw my arms over my head and launched myself into the darkness. The icy water hit my chest like a sledgehammer. I felt the slipstream grab me and thrust me forward.

My head broke the surface seconds later, and I shook water from my ears like a dog. I called Cat's name but heard only silence. My chest felt less painful, and the water was warmer.

Cabin lights glowed around the lagoon.

I listened, my head leaning in the direction of the dock as I headed toward shore, but I heard nothing. Wherever—or whenever—I had arrived, it definitely was not December of 1941.

The sky was clear with its huge moon, and my heart sped up. It sure looked like the night we'd left. I walked out of the water and scanned up and down the beach. Maybe they'd gone straight to the rock where we left our things. I hurried to the spot and stared down in dismay at the bare patch of sand.

No stuff. No twins. No idea.

"Cat! Draggin!" I yelled.

I stood perfectly still, listening with my whole body. If they were here, why would they leave the beach? If I had returned to the right night, where had our things gone? I walked to the end of the spit so I could see up both beaches—the lagoon side and the ocean side to the dock.

Nothing.

I sat down on the point and tried to find a fingernail to chew. I needed to calm down enough to think, but mostly, I wanted to cry.

"Maddy!"

My head popped up. Had I imagined that?

"Maddy!"

It sounded like Cat.

"Cat!" I jumped up and looked around. Out in the lagoon, I saw two heads bobbing along on the water. "Cat! Draggin!" I raced down the beach and waded out to meet them. Cat and I threw our arms around each other, laughing with relief.

"What happened?" Cat and I asked each other at the exact same moment.

Cat went first. "We floated past you, then went back to the point, but you weren't there. We figured you'd gone on, so we swam out to the rock together, dove in, and here we are. I think we barely made it in time, though. The water had started to slow down. Right, Draggin?" He nodded.

"What happened to you?" Cat asked me.

"I called and called for you when you went past me, but I couldn't see you or hear you. I thought you must have made it, so I dove in, too."

I exhaled loudly. Relief drained the adrenalin from my body, leaving me exhausted. "So now the question is, where are we? Or *when* are we?" I asked.

"What do you mean? We're back," Cat said.

I shook my head. "I don't think so. Our stuff isn't where we left it. Come on." I led the way back to the rock and the bare patch of sand. "See?"

Cat laughed and pointed a few feet away to the correct rock, where the clothes, bags, and shoes, were exactly as we'd left them three days ago.

Or was it three days ago? I grabbed Draggin's wrist and checked the display on his watch: *12:18 a.m., August 16.* I showed Cat, nearly wrenching Draggin's arm off. No time had elapsed here; we dove in, floated into the lagoon, and walked out again.

I couldn't stop smiling.

We changed quickly into our dry clothes. Draggin emerged from behind a tree with a huge grin on his face. "I can hear you again!" he said, pointing to his ears.

A brief argument erupted over which tree marked Malila's favourite spot. Things didn't look exactly the same, but when we finally decided between two firs, I began to dig with a large oyster shell. It took only a few minutes to get the hole over a foot deep. Then I used my hands in the moist, cool sand as I was afraid to hit the jar with the shell—assuming we found it.

"I feel it!" I cried. In seconds, I pulled an old mason jar from the hole. All three of us took turns to loosen the lid, but at last, I opened the jar and slid out a folded piece of paper. I scanned the page quickly. "They made it!" I nearly yelled. "The Tagawas got away!"

We popped up from our knees, jumping up and down with our arms around each other—a three-person merry-go-round.

"Let me see the letter," Cat said. As I held it out to her, car beams swung toward us: late night partiers perhaps, or midnight swimmers. Either way, we didn't want to be seen in case it was someone we knew. Or, more importantly, someone who knew our parents.

I stuffed the letter into my bag. We dove into the trees and made our way back to the road through the forest.

We walked as quickly as our exhausted legs would allow—our final dregs of energy carrying each of us home and no further. When we parted at Cat and Draggin's driveway, we agreed to meet at their house first thing in the morning to read the whole letter together.

I couldn't find the strength to climb through the window, and Mom always left the front door unlocked, so I tiptoed down the hall, carefully avoided the creaky spot, and slipped into my room. I kicked Pillow Maddy out of bed, changed into my pyjamas, and was asleep as soon as my head hit the pillow.

The sun finally pushed my eyelids up just before nine thirty. I lay still, letting the memories of my adventure roll over me in waves. What had happened to the Tagawas once they got away from Cortes? How strange to think they'd lived a whole lifetime since last night. Maybe I'd Google Yoshi Tagawa and find out that he really did become a famous Hollywood director. I smiled at the thought.

I sat up and grabbed my bag from the floor. The letter wasn't on top where I'd put it. I dumped the contents on the bed and went through everything carefully, but I couldn't find the letter. My heart sank as I pictured it lying on the road somewhere between here and the lagoon. I dressed hastily and threw open my bedroom door to go search for it.

And there it was, in the hands of my grandma, sitting alone at the kitchen table.

"Hey, Grandma." I tried to keep my voice calm.

"Good morning, Dear. Do you know anything about this letter? I found it lying in the hallway. It's dated December 26, 1941."

I thought fast. I hadn't actually read the letter—had barely skimmed it. I didn't even know if it mentioned me or not. I hurried around the table, sat down beside Grandma, and glanced at the letter. I didn't see my name.

"I found it in a jar at the beach." That was the truth. I exhaled and read the letter over Grandma's shoulder:

> *Dear Travellers, (Malila said to only use her name and mine, just in case!)*
>
> *The family (you know who) got away safely. I can't tell you where they are headed, but Malila says they are still in a lot of danger. Everything got pretty "crazy" at the end. (You know who I mean!) He actually grabbed Mr. T and bonked him a good one on the head, and he was trying to convince people to help him, but then Malila walked up behind him while every-one yelled at each other, and she pushed him right off the dock into the water! He can't swim, so there was a big fuss getting him out and that's when Y grabbed his dad and practically carried him onto the boat*

*on account of Mr. T being groggy with his hurt head. So Y had to drive the boat, but they got away and crazy-you-know-who was too upset about almost drowning to bother chasing them. Malila and her kin are going to take care of the farm. She bought it, you know. For one dollar. It's all writ up, legal. But she'll sell it back for fifty cents, she says, or even a huckleberry pie. Well, I reckon the only way I'll get to see you again will be when we meet in our dreams. I'll meet you at the lagoon.*

*Your friend,*

*Newt*

Grandma turned to look at me with a strange expression on her face.

"What is it, Grandma?" I asked with a wince.

"I was thinking about your grandpa. You know, when he was a boy, no one used his real name for several years. They called him 'Newt.' I'd forgotten about that."

My mouth dropped open. Newt?

Grandma tapped the letter gently. "And this. During our entire marriage, every time we had to spend a night apart, he would tell me that he'd meet me in our dreams. Every time." She looked down at the letter again. "Where did you say you found this, Madison?"

"By the lagoon," I said quietly. The hair was standing up on the back of my neck.

Grandma took off her reading glasses and cupped my chin in her hand. I watched emotions flash across her face the way northern lights pulse through the sky. Finally, she spoke. "He always believed in magic," she said softly, then got up and left the kitchen.

The birds chirped outside as I stared at the letter. I folded the yellowed sheet as gently as I could and carried it to my room. I slid it under my pillow, patted it twice, and whispered, "See you at the lagoon, Grandpa."

Then I went to Grant's office where he was already at work. I tapped twice on his door, and he turned to look at me.

"Yes, Maddy?" he asked.

"I was wondering if you could help me do some research. There's a family I want to look up . . ." I held my breath for a second, but then relaxed when he smiled at me. Little crinkly lines appeared around the corners of his mouth and eyes that I'd never noticed before.

"Sure, Maddy," he said. "Come on in."

Dear Reader,

Thank you for sharing this adventure with me. I hope you enjoyed it. I wanted you to know a few things about *Full Moon Lagoon.*

First, the Tagawa family are characters of fiction. Their story is not meant to reflect that of the Nakatsui family who lived on Cortes Island until 1942.

However, all the facts and dates about the Japanese Internment are true. If you would like to know more about the internment camps, I recommend that you read this book:

*A Child in Prison Camp* by Shizuye Takashima (Tundra Books, 1971)

The legend of the messenger in the lagoon is also fiction, but the Coast Salish tradition has many wonderful legends. If you would like to read some of these, I recommend this book:

> *Kwulasulwut: Stories from the Coast Salish* by Ellen White (Author), David Neel (Illustrator)

Hopefully, you and I will meet in person one day . . . maybe at the Lagoon?

Monica Nawrocki

## Gratitude

First and foremost, thank you, Shanny, for every little thing.

Special thanks to Hannah Hansed for the title, *Full Moon Lagoon;* to Tim Tamishiro for letting me steal "the Differents"; to Chelsea Badger for helpful insight into Deaf culture; and to Jane McDonald for inspiring sketches that led to more.

The research for this book was done almost exclusively at/through the main branch of the Vancouver Public Library. I'm grateful to David Guthrie, Tara Warkentin, the Cortes Island Museum, and June Cameron for books, notes, assistance, a vintage map, and some great stories.

Thanks to Coreen Boucher, Filipe Figueira, Norm Gibbons, and Rex Weyler for your editing expertise. I offer my heartfelt appreciation to all of my readers, through draft after draft: from the members of the grade five to seven class of 2011 at the Cortes Island School whose early feedback shaped the story significantly, to the final proofreaders, and everyone in between—Cindy Chouinard, Frank Chouinard, Dayna Davis, Bruce Ellingsen, Ginny Ellingsen, Elinore Harwood, Yvonne Kipp, Carrie Saxifrage, and Faith Wyse.

Abundant gratitude to Ambrose Books: *Full Moon Lagoon* would not exist without your support.

Finally, to Lisa Gibbons, my favourite artist, and my friend: thank you!

Monica

## About the Author

Monica Nawrocki lives on Cortes Island, where Full Moon Lagoon takes place. She is a substitute teacher, but the fun kind. Visit her at www.monicanawrocki.com

CPSIA information can be obtained
at www.ICGtesting.com
Printed in the USA
LVOW13*1449071216

516242LV00012B/210/P